The Dream King's Daughter

James Bow

The Dream King's Daughter

James Bow

Cover by: Alisha Souillet
at Bibliofic Designs
www.biblioficdesigns.com

Earthenhouse Incorporated
Kitchener, Ontario, Canada

THE DREAM KING'S DAUGHTER

First edition. April 2025.

Book design by: James Bow
Cover design by: Alisha Souillet @ Bibliofic Designs
Wheat sheaf divider icon courtesy vecteezy.com

ISBN: 978-1-7750844-3-3 (Paperback)
ISBN: 978-1-7750844-4-0 (eBook)

The author wishes to thank the Ontario Arts Council and
the Government of Ontario for their support:

Published by Earthenhouse Incorporated, through IngramSpark, in
Canada

Earthenhouse Incorporated
10-525 Highland Road West, Suite 252
Kitchener, ON
N2M 5P4

www.bowjamesbow.ca

For Wayfinder and Eleanor.

About time we got this updated.

TABLE OF CONTENTS

PROLOGUE

"Your name is Aurora Kelso. Not Perrault. Kelso."

"Kelso," Aurora muttered.

"You have lived in Cooper's Corners all your life. You
have no mother. You have no father. There is only Aunt
Matron."

"Aunt Matron."

"Forget me."

"I... forget..."

A persistent light winked Aurora slowly back to con-
sciousness. She snorted and fruitlessly tried to flick it
away. She opened her eyes and shut them again at the
sudden bright blindness. She raised her head and looked
around, groggy. Her mouth was dry and tasted terrible.

She could barely take in what her eyes were telling
her. They were on a black ribbon ploughing through a sea
of yellow, the only car on the road. The horizon ahead of
them was dark, but the clouds glowed like mountains.

Beside her, her mother hunched over the steering
wheel, staring ahead with the glazed look that suggested

extreme concentration in the face of a desperate need for caffeine.

This isn't right, thought a small clear voice deep in the addled confines of Aurora's brain. *The sun peeking over the horizon behind me is sunrise. We've driven all night. We're still driving.*

"Wh-where?" she croaked. She strained against her seat belt. Her joints ached from sleeping upright. "M-mom, wh-where—?"

Her mom's cheeks were wet, and she cleared her nose with a sniff. She gave Aurora a quick look and adjusted the controls, and the side-view mirror dipped, taking the sun out of Aurora's eyes.

"Just rest, honey. Jus…just go to sleep, and rest."

She placed a hand over Aurora's eyes…

And Aurora slept for three and a half years.

CHAPTER ONE:
THE SEA OF TASSELS

WHEN AURORA KELSO CAME TO REFILL THE
Hendersons' coffee cups at table six, she could see
that Britney had been having that nightmare again.

The Hendersons' four-year-old daughter sat by the window, playing with her Barbie doll while her parents looked out at the dusty August wheat fields and finished the dregs of their breakfasts.

The kitchen could be heard through the window behind the counter. Eggs sizzled, and the coffee maker gurgled while Aunt Matron scraped the grease trap. At the back of the room, a slosh of water came as Polk washed the dishes. Country music played on the radio.

The stools along the counter were all empty except for one. Most of the locals came as families these days, big men in plaid shirts with their wives and children. They chose the booths along the picture window that looked out across the highway and onto Cooper Farm. Even the teenaged farmhands clustered in groups of four or five. Not that there was much jostling for seats. The diner could seat twice as many people as those who lived in the hamlet, and the number of people who drove up the road each week could be counted on one hand.

Britney looked up from her Barbie doll and giggled as her father made faces at her.

She's not even thinking of the nightmare she had last night, Aurora thought. *She hardly even remembers it. But it's there, waiting. It's going to come again.*

When Britney looked up into Aurora's eyes, Aurora saw it.

A flurry of legs, a scrabble of claws, the slimy, green skin. A great leap of fangs arches down. Britney screams—

Aurora gripped her coffee carafe and swayed a little. She closed her eyes and let the dream pass through her. It was only a dream, after all. But try telling that to Britney. She approached the table with a smile. "More coffee, everyone?"

Mr. Henderson beamed and held up his cup. "Yes, please."

Mrs. Henderson passed hers over. "Me, too."

Aurora turned her bright smile on the girl. "And what would the little lady like for dessert?"

Mr. Henderson grinned at Britney. "What do you think, pixie?"

The girl sat so upright her blonde locks bounced. "Ice cream!"

Her father's grin widened. "Are you sure now?"

The girl's head bobbed.

Mr. Henderson nodded to Aurora. "Ice cream it is, Miss Kelso!"

"Well." Aurora set her carafe aside and clapped her

hands together. "Maybe somebody would like to pick out their favourite flavour?"

The girl kicked her legs happily then looked quickly at her father. He smiled and nodded. Britney hopped from her seat and followed Aurora to the ice cream stand.

But rather than haul Britney up to show her the flavours, Aurora knelt so that her face was level with Britney's.

"Britney," she said, keeping her voice low. "Have you been having that nightmare again?"

Britney's smile vanished. She nodded. Her lower lip trembled.

"You did what I told you, right?" said Aurora. "You imagined a door with a lot of locks?"

Britney sniffed. "But it came through the window."

Aurora looked away. Barriers never worked. Running away never worked. They always found a way through and ran faster. There was only one way left to deal with this.

She turned back to Britney, "Okay. You want to make Mr. Scaly go away for good."

Britney nodded vigorously.

"You've already imagined a fence, right?" said Aurora, "And it came true?"

Britney nodded. "But he jumped over it," she mumbled.

"You've already imagined a door," Aurora continued. "So, you know that you can imagine whatever you want in the dream, and it's right there in front of you. Right?"

Britney's brow furrowed, but she nodded.

"So, I want you to imagine..." *What can I say? The kid's only four years old. It didn't seem right to be giving a four-year-old a gun, even in her dreams.* "A bicycle pump."

Britney tilted her head and gave Aurora a baleful look from under her eyebrows.

"Trust me." Aurora squeezed Britney's shoulder gently. "A bicycle pump... with a big wad of gum at the end, so that Mr. Scaly's teeth sink in and... get stuck."

A smile spread across Britney's face. Already Aurora could see how the dream would go. Mr. Scaly would leap, teeth clamping down, while Britney raised the nozzle of her bicycle pump like a dragonslayer. And the teeth would go... *scrunch*... and there would be Mr. Scaly, dangling off the nozzle, feebly trying to pry his mouth loose. Slimy claws catching and sticking to the big wad of chewing gum.

And Britney would clasp the bicycle pump and begin pumping. And Mr. Scaly would puff up like a balloon, making muffled, desperate grunts as his eyes bugged out like a blowfish. He'd puff bigger and bigger until his skin paled and creaked. Then Britney would pause. He would stare at her. He'd make one last pleading squeal as Britney reached for the pump and shoved it down hard...

Aurora closed her eyes at the sudden pop. Britney laughed. Aurora almost felt sorry for Mr. Scaly. Almost.

Definitely don't give this kid a gun, even in her dreams.

She hugged Britney and hefted her up to the glass. "Now, what flavour would you like?"

"Chock-lit," said Britney. And smiled.

Aurora whipped off her apron as she entered the kitchen and strode over to the sink to wash her hands.

"I'm on break, Matron," she called.

"You don't have to shout it, dearie." Matron looked up over the sizzle of the grill. "And you're not on break yet. Not until the Hobsons' eggs are up."

"Yeah, I know." Aurora smiled at the sturdy woman with the greying red hair. Their eyes met.

The wind blows the surf against the beach. Palms wave in the breeze and the sky is a cobalt dome. The hot sand rubs between Matron's toes, but she smiles as she walks with purpose. Up ahead is a marguerita stand.

Aurora let the images wash over her and soothe her, even though she didn't really need it. What was she going to do once Matron decided to retire and get that Florida bungalow?

"But those eggs won't be up for a few minutes, will they?" she asked. When Matron refused to answer, she added, "Until then, I'm on break."

"You could do the dishes, you know," said Matron as Aurora reached for the back door.

"That's Polk's job." Aurora glanced at the sink, a mountain range of dishes and bubbles. "Where is that slacker?" She shoved open the back door, and the midsummer heat hit her. She marched down the steps.

She found Polk, Matron's foster son, lying down in the gravel parking lot, on the concrete lip that protected the battered stairwell from flooding the basement storage. He was stretched out on his back, an arm curled behind his head for a pillow, and his baseball cap planted over his face, snoring.

She stood over top of him, her hands on her hips. "What are you doing out here, slacker?"

The snoring stopped, but Polk didn't move. "I'm on break, blondie."

She kicked him. He fell into the stairwell.

He landed lightly on his feet and jumped up over the parapet. The gravel scrunched underfoot as he stood in front of her, arms folded, cap on his dirty brown hair, a one-sided grin on his face. "What's up?"

"There were a lot of dishes in the sink last time I looked."

"There were still eggs to be served last time *I* looked."

"I'll go back if you go back," said Aurora.

"Now who's the slacker?"

They glared at each other for a long moment, each waiting for the other to blink. Then, the tension broke as both snorted with laughter at the same time.

"C'mon." He nodded to the back wall of the diner.

As she looked up at him, their eyes met. Instinctively, Aurora braced herself.

Polk walks across the gravel lot behind the diner and pushes aside the stalks of wheat as he enters the neighbouring field. He grins as he wades into the waving sea of golden brown. The blue skies stretch on forever, and he shields his face from the sun.

And you say that you want to get away from all this, thought Aurora. *Liar.*

But as Polk broke the connection and leaned against the wall, Aurora reflected that he was, frankly, a relief. For the three years since she became a teenager here at Cooper's Corners, it was getting so she couldn't look any of the other boys in the eye. It was just too embarrassing.

But Polk had none of that. No crass thoughts about wet T-shirts. His dreams consisted of nothing but the ground on which he stood.

You talk big, she thought, *but you don't dream about anywhere or anything else. I like you.*

"Fine," she said, following him. "But call me blondie one more time, and you'll regret it."

"Sure thing, blond—" He chuckled at her as she glared.

Aurora leaned on the sun-bleached siding and stared out across the fields. The wheat rolled like golden surf in the hot, dusty wind. The late August sunlight settled on them like a warm cloak. She scuffed the gravel with the toe of her shoe. Then her toe hit something. She looked down.

Knocked loose by her foot was a small, flat stone, dark where the gravel was white. She frowned and picked it up.

There was heft to it, like a baseball. It narrowed from half an inch thick on one side to almost a knife's point, but there were no sharp edges to cut her. Her palm and forefinger curved around the thick side perfectly.

It was a skipping stone. She knew it was a skipping stone, though they were miles away from any water to skip it on. She could picture herself leaning into the throw, bringing her arm around, letting the stone go, and watching it catch the air like a sail and then meet the water along its smooth, flat end, arching back into the air again and again and again.

But before her, only a sea of tassels waved.

Polk bent down and snapped a stalk of wild grass growing by the base of the building. He put one end of the stalk between his teeth and started chewing.

Aurora rolled her eyes. "Polk!"

The grass stalk arched up. "What?"

"Take that out of your mouth!" She snatched at it, but Polk ducked away. "I swear, if city folks see you like that, they may as well pose next to you for photographs."

He shrugged. "They could if they paid me a dollar."

She sighed. "Only a dollar?"

Then, movement caught Aurora's eye, and she looked past Polk at the strip of asphalt that disappeared in the distance. A cloud of dust was rising at the road's vanishing point.

"Truck," she said.

Polk leaned back and closed his eyes. "Hmm... It'll be a B-train, double long semi, white, with a grain logo, and it won't stop."

"No points if it doesn't stop." Aurora levered herself from the wall and stepped out into the gravel lot, watching the growing cloud like a hawk. The whine of its engine and the growl of its wheels grew as it shaped itself into a dark cab and two points of light. Aurora walked to the edge of the wheat field, keeping the truck in sight until it passed behind the diner and roared past.

"Well?" said Polk when she came back.

"B-train," she grumbled. "Double long semi. White. With a grain logo."

His eyes stayed closed, and his lips quirked up. "And it didn't stop."

"I told you: no points for that. No one stops in the middle of Saskatchewan. They're either heading for Alberta or Saskatoon. You don't deserve an extra point for that."

"They could stop sometimes," he said. "Call of nature and the like."

"And seeing as we're on the prairies, I'm being extra generous, giving you a point for the grain logo."

"Four points, then," said Polk.

"Three."

"Four!"

"Three!"

"Okay."

She shook her head at heaven and leaned on the siding beside him. After a while, she said, "What are you going to do with your life, Polk?"

He shrugged, a quick jerk of his shoulders. "Well, you know me. I've got plans. I'm going to see the world. Join a circus. Take a computer course and make it rich in Redmond. I can't wash dishes for the rest of my life."

Yeah, right. She bit back the next question: *what's keeping you?*

"What about you?" he asked casually. "What are you going to do with your life now that you're almost sixteen?"

She made a face at him. Lately, he'd often mentioned that she was "almost sixteen," reminding her yet again that she wasn't sixteen yet, and he was almost seventeen, in fact. Like that made any difference. Except that it did.

"I'll be sixteen in five days, twerp," she said. But as she shoved aside the taunt and focused on the question, she frowned. "I don't know," she said at last. "Something. Anything. It's not a life, serving coffee in some country diner. It's something temporary. It's got to change..." Her voice trailed off.

It's got to change because it's wrong, said a voice in the deepest part of her mind.

"You seem okay with your life here," said Polk.

"Aunt Matron's okay," said Aurora. "She takes care of me, and we get along. But she's not a mom, though."

Mom. The word echoed briefly.

"And there's nothing to *do* here," she said, with more force than she'd intended. But the words had popped a cork and more came flowing out. "It's like I'm a prisoner!" She blinked. *Where did that thought come from?*

And just like that, the impulse to question hit a brick wall.

Polk arched an eyebrow. "A prisoner? Matron got you locked in your bedroom, spinning gold from wheat?"

Aurora sighed. Her bedroom door didn't even lock. "You know what I mean."

She felt the heft of the stone in her hand again. She gave it a quick glance, then looked out at the sea of tassels. She stepped forward and threw it.

It arched as in her imagination, cleared the driveway, and sailed over the tops of the wheat. It curved down...

The wheat splashed. Black erupted from the sea of gold. A crow, cawing angrily, rose from the waves. The stone arched back into the air, came down again a few feet away, and burst the wheat a second time as another crow soared and flapped away to the horizon.

The stone fell a third time and disappeared among the stalks.

Polk's arms dropped to his sides. The grass stalk fell from his mouth. "Two birds with one stone? Great shot!"

"But I didn't mean to hit them," she exclaimed. "They were just there!"

"You got lucky, I guess?"

Maybe. But why should I feel lucky that I hit two crows?

Movement caught her eye. She looked down the highway. Another cloud of dust was approaching. She pushed down her strange worry and nudged Polk. "Truck!"

He leaned back and closed his eyes. "Hmm..." He frowned. "Tough one..."

She blinked. She'd never seen him uncertain before.

"Uh..." He drew himself up. "Double rig, fourteen wheels. Red cab, white body, no logo. And it won't stop."

"No points if it doesn't stop," she said automatically. She strode out to the wheat field, keeping her eye on the road as the dust cloud shaped itself into multiple points of light. She frowned. The cab was black, not red, as was the container, single, not double. Ten wheels. She grinned. He'd gotten this one *way* wrong.

Then her grin faded. The truck *was* stopping.

Her mouth dropped open, but there was no mistaking it. The whine of the engine rolled lower. The brakes rumbled. As she stared agape, the truck moved behind one side of the diner and didn't emerge from the other. By the wall, Polk had opened his eyes and was blinking.

Aurora ran to him. "It stopped!"

He turned to the back door. "I know."

Aurora yanked open the back door, and they both bolted through at the same time—or tried to. There was a brief struggle as they squeezed past each other and burst into the kitchen.

"There you are!" Matron scraped grease off the grill and into the trough. "I served the Hobsons while you were out."

"Thanks, but—" Aurora began.

The bell above the door jangled. Matron looked out through the cook's window. "We've got customers."

"I know." Aurora pulled on her apron.

Matron frowned. "Not a local."

"Where's my notepad?" Aurora patted the pockets of her apron frantically.

"You never needed one before," said Matron, wiping down her cooking utensils.

"It's not a regular," said Aurora. "I've never heard his order before." She darted into the dining area.

The new customer was easy to spot just by looking at the other customers. He'd reoriented them like another gravity. The Hobsons were eating quietly but casting curious glances over their shoulders. As the Hendersons gathered Britney's entourage of toys and eased the girl out the door, both parents looked back occasionally to where a man like a black hole sat on one of the stools by the counter, reading a menu.

Aurora grabbed a mug and dragged the carafe from the coffee maker. It made a sound like a knife sliding from its sheath. She shook the strangeness of this sudden simile from her head and pulled herself together. Walking along the counter space, she eyed the new customer.

He was a big man like truckers should be, dressed in black denim jeans and a black short-sleeved shirt with a collar. His muscled arms were matted with black hair, and he had thick black hair and a black beard.

And he probably likes his coffee black, she added to herself. Without asking, she filled the mug and set it in front of him. "See anything you like?" she prompted.

The man looked up. His eyes met hers. The whites of his eyes were black.

"You," he said.

Crows.

Aurora staggered back into the cash register. She tried to regain control of her knees, but they didn't belong to her body anymore.

There was a crash in the kitchen. Matron burst through the door, waving her spatula like a club. "Aurora!"

Aurora fell. The coffee sloshed over the carafe and scalded her fingers before shattering on the countertop, but she didn't notice. She was out before she hit the floor.

Aurora dreamed of the last time she'd seen Lake Winnipeg.

She was twelve, several months away from turning thirteen. She sat on a boulder, kicking at stones underfoot, while waves lapped at the shore. The early March sky was the colour of unpainted canvas. The north breeze flicked Aurora's blonde hair into her face. She pulled up the zipper of her windbreaker.

"Find what you're looking for, honey?" asked her mom.

Aurora looked up. Her mother flashed her a grin as she sat on a wave-battered stump. She had her hands thrust into her jacket, and the wind was blowing her blonde hair in front of her face. She'd sat with Aurora, looking across the waves as though waiting for a lost love.

Aurora said nothing. She returned her mother's quick smile, then returned to her close examination of the stones beneath her feet. They clacked and skittered. Then she found it.

It was a round, flat stone, dark and mottled, while the others around it were white. Aurora picked it up. It had the heft of a baseball and narrowed from half an inch thick on one side to almost a knife's edge at the other, but there were no sharp edges to cut her. Her palm and forefinger curved around the thick side perfectly. Aurora cupped it in her palm, clasped it, then stood up. She eyed the northern horizon and took a deep breath.

She leaned into the shot, swinging the stone in a side-arm throw. It left her fingers, spinning, and caught the air like a sail. It met the water along its smooth, flat end, arching back into the air again. Aurora counted the splashes. She clenched her fist and smiled when she reached eight, and the stone finally disappeared.

Her mother clapped. "A new world record!"

She rolled her eyes. "Hardly."

"Who's to know?" said her mother. "It's not like they keep records on that sort of thing."

"Actually, they do. Some guy in Pennsylvania managed to get eighty-eight." Aurora shoved her hands in her pockets.

"Aurora?" The tone of her mother's voice made Aurora turn. Her mother stood up from the stump. "What's bothering you? You've been...withdrawn these past few days. I know that's the default state of a teenager, but you're only twelve, kid. And, besides, I'm a school counsellor with a psychology degree. I know the difference between normal teenagerhood and when something's bothering you. Please tell me."

Aurora sighed. "Mom, nothing's wrong."

"Problems with your teachers?"

"No."

"Problems with Anne?"

"No!" Anne was her best friend.

"Problems with... boys?"

"Mom! No!…Well…"

Her mother drew herself up, bracing herself for this moment. *But it's not what she thinks,* thought Aurora. *If only.*

"You know that boy at school, Roger?" Aurora began.

"The bully you fought?" Her mother nodded. "I know I shouldn't condone violence, but that was still very brave of you."

Aurora's breath caught. "Er…no. It wasn't. It…you don't understand, I…" She halted and breathed deep.

This was it. It all had to come out. She had to tell somebody, or she'd explode. And her mother was the only person left she could talk to. "You see—"

A sound like the squeak of a rusty gate made her turn. On the branch of a stunted tree at the edge of the beach, a crow cocked its head to one side, then the other. It cawed. The north wind picked up, and Aurora shivered.

She thought: *It's just a bird.*

A bird looking at me.

A bird's got eyes, she thought. *It can look at whatever it wants. It's a free country.*

But a bird shouldn't look at me with intent. What was

it that lawyer guy said on that television show? Malice aforethought? The look was that intense.

She was about to turn away, dismiss the crow from her mind when she heard her mom shout. A stone sailed over Aurora's head and struck the branch. The crow flew up, screeching.

"Get out of here!" her mother yelled, reaching for another stone. "Go on, get!" She threw the other rock, and the crow dodged out of the way. It aimed for the sky and took off, cawing.

"Mom!" Aurora shouted when she got her voice back. "Mom, why are—?" Then she looked at her mother. "Mom, what's wrong?"

"What? Nothing. Nothing's wrong. Let's go home."

Aurora stood her ground. "Mom?"

Her mother walked carefully over the stones while keeping one eye on the clouds. "Nothing's wrong, honey. It's just that it's late, and it's getting cold."

Aurora was about to protest when she heard cawing above and looked up. A dotted line of black shapes was weaving across the grey sky. Crows. Flying in a steady stream, calling out to each other as they migrated east.

East?

Her mother reached out for her. "C'mon, honey, don't argue, please. Let's go home."

Aurora hesitated. Her mother snatched her hand and pulled, almost roughly.

"Mom!" Aurora stumbled alongside her to the car. "Seriously, what's wrong?"

"Nothing's wrong, honey." Her mother was looking at the sky.

She let go of Aurora's hand as they reached the car and opened the side door for her. As Aurora bent to slide inside, a *caw* made her look up.

The crow was watching her from the branch again.

She got in and slammed the door.

Her mother started the car and drove off in a spray of gravel.

When Aurora got home, her mother put on Aurora's favourite movie, *The Princess Bride*, and made popcorn and cocoa. But then her mother went to her bedroom and shut the door. Aurora heard her talking to someone.

She set her popcorn aside and crept down the hall to the bedroom door. She put her ear to the door, but her mom's voice stayed muffled.

"...a problem...He may have found us..."

More muffled conversation, a shifting of floor boards. Aurora could picture her mother on the phone, standing by the bedside table, turning slowly, the cord twisting around her.

"Don't think I was followed...You say he has eyes everywhere..."

More mutters, then. "I just don't know what to do! I know! He can't—!" Then more quietly, "But where do I go?"

There was a long, listening silence in the bedroom.

"You're sure you can keep her safe?" said her mother at last. "But you're in the middle of nowhere!"

More silence, then. "Do you promise? Matron, I'm not

going anywhere unless you promise! If I'm going to trust you with my daughter, then you have to swear it! On whatever it is you use as a holy book, swear it!"

Another listening silence, then, "Okay. Okay, I'll tell her."

She hung up. Footsteps approached from inside the bedroom. Aurora thought about racing back to the couch but decided instead to wait, arms folded, as her mother opened the door.

Her mother gasped to see her standing there.

"What's going on, Mom?"

Aurora saw a parade of emotions stream across her mother's face—shock, horror, shame —before her mother got herself back under control and gave her daughter a small smile as she matched Aurora folding her arms across her own chest.

"Hey, honey," she said. "Want to make a little money?"

Aurora opened her mouth, then stopped. After a moment, she closed her mouth. "Okay. Tell me more."

"I just got a call from your Aunt Matron," said her mother.

Aurora nodded and didn't mention that she hadn't heard the phone ring. Aunt Matron was a kindly older woman. Though she had red hair, she hardly looked like her mom's sister. She was a good source of gifts whenever she visited and always included a cheque when birthday or Christmas cards arrived. But where did she live again?

"She's been caught short," her mother went on. "One of her hired hands up and left."

Saskatchewan, Aurora thought. *Northern Saskatchewan.*

The hired hand probably went crazy and made a mad dash for civilization.

Aloud, she said, "That's too bad."

"She asked if you could come out and help, for spring break, while she looks for a replacement," her mom went on. "It's win-win. She'd love to see you, and she'll pay the usual wage. How often do you get paid to spend some time with one of your relatives?"

There is that. Aurora looked up at her mother. "And this has nothing to do with why you were so upset back at the lake?"

"What?" said her mother quickly. "N-no! It's just… helping family, okay? You can do that, can't you? And make a little money on the side?"

Aurora nodded. *You're not going to tell me why you're so scared, are you? You're a liar, and worst of all, you think you're doing this for my benefit. Well, visiting Aunt Matron might be a good consolation prize. If I play along, maybe I can figure out what's going on. Maybe I can wear Matron down and get an explanation.*

She smiled at her mother, reached out and brushed her cheek, knocking the glass spirit ball beads that dangled from her mother's ear—folk art that supposedly protected against bad dreams. "Sure!"

"Pack a bag, honey. We'll grab a bite to eat on the road."

Aurora blinked. "We're going *now*?"

Her mother beamed. "Yup!" As though they were on their way to Disney World. And she sent Aurora to her room to pack.

As Aurora put clothes in a suitcase, she thought about

arguing or even throwing a fit, but at the back of her mind, a little voice told her to play along. There was something about the tension in her mother's shoulders that made her keep her head down. To do otherwise would be like putting a match to a balloon full of gasoline.

So she packed up a week's change of clothes, a bunch of her favourite books *(Aunt Matron didn't have cable!)* plus Freddy, the teddy bear that she'd publicly sworn she was too old for but had never deigned to recycle, and hauled the suitcase out of the house and to her mother's SUV.

Her mother loaded the suitcase into the back of the vehicle and hurried Aurora into the car. She kept on looking at the trees, but there were no waiting crows. Finally, her mother piled in behind the steering wheel and snapped on her seatbelt. "Ready?"

"Are you?" asked Aurora, one eyebrow raised.

Her mother took a breath and held it. "No," she said at last and turned the key in the ignition. Aurora was pressed into her seat as the car shot out of the driveway. The glass spirit ball dangling from the rear-view mirror was pulled almost horizontal.

"Mom!"

"Sorry," said her mother, and slowed down.

They pulled into the first McDonald's drive-through and bought Big Macs to eat on their laps as they drove. Traffic was heavy as they eased onto the Perimeter Highway, but it moved. As the cars, trucks and SUVs surrounded them, Aurora heard her mother breathing a sigh of relief, but the tension didn't ease from her shoulders, even as they pulled onto the Trans-Canada.

They had the radio on, and they drove on without talking. Aurora kept her ear open for the news in case some secret tsunami was on its way to crush Winnipeg behind them.

They pushed westward. The rocky land of the Canadian Shield gave way to pasture and then grain fields. They chased the sun as it disappeared over the horizon and kept driving as the farmhouse lights winked off and the interior of their car flashed dark to bright in the headlights of oncoming trucks. The radio stations gave way to static.

"Shall I put on some music, honey?" asked her mother. For the next hour, they listened to Mozart. Aurora curled her legs beneath her, rested her cheek against the headrest and stared out at the blackness, flecked with distant specks of light.

Mom pushed a button on the dash, changing to a new channel. The audio started softly, with the sound of rushing surf.

Then, her mother's voice washed over the car from the speakers.

"I'd like you to take deep, slow breaths. Imagine that with each breath, you are putting all your tension, all your stress, into your lungs and breathing them out of your mouth. With each breath, your eyelids are getting heavier."

Aurora's eyelids fluttered.

"Keep your breathing slow and steady," continued her mother's recorded voice. "With each breath, you are falling deeper and deeper asleep."

And Aurora slipped into a deep sleep. She would have been surprised if she hadn't been so sleepy.

"Your name is Aurora Kelso. Not Perrault. Kelso."

A hand clapped on Aurora's shoulder. She woke with a gasp and then looked around frantically. She was standing in the middle of the diner. Tom Hobson held her by the shoulder with one hand and had taken the coffee carafe out of her hand with the other. "Careful, there, young lady! You almost spilled your coffee. Does Matron work you like a slave night and day?"

Aurora pulled herself together and looked around at the diner. It was a normal end of the lunch hour.

The dark man was nowhere to be seen.

"You were out on your feet," Mr. Hobson added.

In her mind's eye, Aurora burst out of the controlling blanket and wriggled free.

Her mouth dropped open. "How long was I asleep?"

CHAPTER TWO:
THE MURDER OF CROWS

AURORA PUSHED OPEN THE DOOR TO THE kitchen and set the coffee carafe down with a sloshing clatter. "What just happened out there?"

Silence descended in the kitchen, so far as it could. Polk and Matron stared at Aurora over the sounds of running water and sizzling bacon.

Polk glanced from Aurora to Matron. His mouth quirked up. "Oh, wait, is this a game? Let me guess: you served coffee to a lot of customers? What do I win?"

"Quiet, Polk," said Matron. To Aurora, she said, "What are you talking about, dearie?"

Aurora spluttered. *They* had *to know! They'd run out of the kitchen to help her when—*

No, wait, they hadn't. They're still here. They hadn't moved from their posts.

She gripped a countertop, suddenly dizzy. "This is... just...weird."

Polk reached out but stopped about a foot away. "What's weird? What happened?"

"I mean..." Aurora gabbled. "I fall on the floor, and

suddenly I'm *not* on the floor. And the new customer who came in suddenly isn't—"

"Whoa, whoa," said Polk. "Wait: *what* new customer?"

Aurora looked at them, eyes wide. The pieces of the picture came together. She'd waited on a new customer, and suddenly, he wasn't there. Nor was his truck. She remembered collapsing, and suddenly…she hadn't. She remembered Polk and Matron rushing to her rescue, and suddenly, they weren't.

Which meant the new customer and his truck didn't happen. I'm hallucinating. I'm sleepwalking. I'm crazy. Take your pick.

And with Polk and Matron's eyes on her, full of concern, she knew this was not a decision she wanted to make in front of them.

"Um…yeah. Never mind." She picked up the carafe. "When's the next order up?"

The diner was deserted by eight at night, so Aurora, Polk and Matron cleaned up the place early. Aurora wiped down the tables and hauled the garbage out back, all on automatic. Her mind was full of dreams, and the childhood memories they had unlocked. Luckily, she could think and wield a dishcloth at the same time.

They were out the door only five minutes after closing time. Polk and Matron paid only passing attention to the red-gold summer sunset painting the landscape. They'd seen the scenery every day of their lives. The long shadows rippling over top of the wheat, like holes opening and closing in the golden field.

Aurora stood breathing the cooling air. Then she remembered the crows and scanned the tops of the tassels, listening for the beat of wings. Only the breeze whispered in her ears.

She pursed her lips. *Was this part of the dream as well? When exactly had the dream started?*

A screen door creaked open, leading to the apartment over-top the diner the three shared. Polk poked his head out. "Hey, blond—" He grinned at the look she threw him. "You coming in or what?"

Why not ask him?

"Come here," she said, jerking her head.

He crouched behind the protection of the screen door. "I said I was sorry about the blonde joke."

"No, you didn't," said Aurora. "But I'm not going to hit you. I just want to ask you something."

He stepped out from behind the screen door and crept forward, arms raised as if in surrender. Aurora folded her arms impatiently, and he dropped his hands to his sides. "What about?"

"About the break we took this afternoon." She watched his expression. "I threw that stone—"

He chortled. "Yeah, and you hit two crows? That was so cool!"

So, that wasn't part of the dream. Somehow, that's not com-forting. "What did I do, after?"

"Other than cheer?"

"I didn't cheer!"

He flashed his lopsided grin. "Why are you asking me, then?"

She slugged him.

He staggered back, clutching his shoulder. "You said you weren't going to hit me!"

"Not about the blonde joke. Be serious for once! I know the question's silly, but I need an answer! What did I do next?"

"You... Matron called us in. Said the Hobsons' order was up. You went into the diner."

"Did I say anything?"

"Not a thing. I thought you were angry or something."

She looked away. "I see."

"Were you?"

"Was I what?"

"Angry at me? You just clammed up and walked off without a word."

She gave him a tight smile. "Nah...I don't know, Polk, I'm just having a weird day."

He nodded slowly. "Well, don't have too many of those, okay? I'm supposed to be the moody one, around here. I can't handle the competition."

She laughed. "Yeah, okay."

He nodded over his shoulder. "C'mon! Matron's loading up the next season of *Corner Gas*."

Aurora followed Polk up the stairs to Matron's apartment. There, she and Polk sprawled next to Matron on the battered, fluffy couch and they watched their DVD on Matron's aging, wall-mounted widescreen. Popcorn rattled in the microwave. An hour later, Matron turned off the television and hauled herself off the couch, grimacing as her legs protested. "Bedtime, Aurora. I'll straighten up."

Aurora nodded. No argument about staying up later, as Polk slept on the couch. She levered herself up and gave Matron a brief kiss on the cheek. "Good night!"

Polk grabbed a set of blankets from behind the couch and flopped down, wrapping his cocoon around himself in record time. "Night," was his muffled response. Aurora and Matron went to their respective bedrooms. Aurora sat at her wooden desk, finishing off her algebra assignment for correspondence school.

At eleven, she eased into bed, washed, brushed and wearing a long T-shirt. She pulled the covers to her chest and fluffed up the pillows behind her, and then she lay back and stared at the ceiling.

How could I have forgotten my mother?

Two conflicting sets of memories bumped their shopping carts in the aisles of her mind. She remembered growing up with her mother, and she remembered having no parents at all. She remembered going to a real school in St. Boniface and having picnics on the shores of Lake Winnipeg, and she remembered living in Cooper's Corners, in middle-of-nowhere Saskatchewan all her life, coming to Aunt Matron as a young orphan, playing with the village kids, being homeschooled and gradually taking over the waitressing duty until she grew into her life of wiping counters and serving coffee all day, every day.

As she reached back in her mind, the memories of Manitoba flooded her. Summer barbecues. Homework. Roger, the school bully.

She shuddered. Okay, it was a mixed bag, but the tumble of revealed memories told her what was real and what was fake. She'd *had* a mother. She also had an Aunt Matron, and three years of experience living in Cooper's Corners, waiting tables, babysitting Britney. But somehow she'd been made to think that there was no one else *but* Aunt Matron. And as she finally remembered the trip that had taken her from Winnipeg to this place, she had a pretty good idea of who had done this to her.

Confusing the picture was the crow man and the cloud of crows that filled her vision when she had looked him in the eye without Polk and Matron noticing. What was up with that? Had she dreamed it all while sleepwalking?

No, she thought. *Something attacked me. When that black truck arrived today, something—possibly the crow man—pulled me into a dream and tried to grab me. And I reacted by ducking back into a deeper dream, about the day before I came here, breaking the hypnosis that kept me here.*

But how could I do that without anybody noticing? I don't sleepwalk. I don't even sleep.

Tomorrow, she thought, *I'm going into that diner with my eyes open.*

Aurora grabbed the first book off her bedside table, *The Kite Runner,* found her place, and began reading.

She finished the book by midnight, set it down, and picked up the next book on her pile, *A Thousand Splendid Suns.* She adjusted her pillows around her and started in.

Just after one in the morning, she left her bedroom to go pee. Returning to her room, she took up Terry Pratchett's *Small Gods* and started to read. At two-thirty, she set that book aside and turned out the light. She lay in bed and stared at the ceiling.

Around three, she caught the time off the low-light display of her tablet and stared up at the ceiling again.

Her teachers were convinced she was a fast reader; instead, she simply had more time to read than most people. But in the end, there was only so much you could read at one time. If you didn't want to wake up the house around you, you ended up staring at the ceiling, waiting for the sun to rise. And that was when the darkest thoughts started to materialize if you weren't careful.

"Maybe I'm dead," she muttered aloud. And why not? Now that she remembered her past life, she recalled that conversation from three years ago. Death was practically a medical diagnosis...

🌾

"So, Aurora," said Dr. Zane. "You're in perfect health. Is there anything else?"

"Yeah." Aurora couldn't suppress the urge to look around to make sure they were alone, even though the doctor's office was half the size of her bedroom in the house she shared with her mom. She leaned close. "I can't sleep."

The doctor frowned. "You're having trouble sleeping?"

She nodded.

"How long has this been going on?"

She looked into his eyes.

"...And the Nobel prize in medicine," the master of ceremonies shouts, "for his contributions to medical science: Dr. Myron Zane!"

Dr. Zane approaches the podium, carried on the shoul-

ders of his colleagues. The audience chants "Zane! Zane! Zane!"

"Thank you!" he shouts to the cheering masses. "I owe it all to—"

Instead of "the past four months," Aurora said, "A while."

"Everything good at school?"

She stopped herself from rolling her eyes. He'd ask that about a hangnail. "Fine."

He blinked. "Everything good at home?"

"It's fine!"

"Your bed uncomfortable?"

She shook her head.

"Something worrying you?"

Other than the fact that I don't sleep and that I see people's dreams whenever I look them in the eye? "No."

He leaned back in his chair. "Many people have trouble getting to sleep, Aurora. You're probably putting too much pressure on yourself. It's a bit of a Catch-22. I can give you some relaxation exercises you can try as you go to bed..."

He droned on. Aurora stared at his steepled fingers. *This is going nowhere. But how can it go anywhere when I haven't told him the true extent of the problem?*

It had started slowly. In the days after that first alarming bleed and those deeply embarrassing conversations about pads and tampons, Aurora had tossed and turned at night. She didn't think there was anything unusual about that. In the stress of those days, of course she'd have trouble getting to sleep. And she wasn't tired when she woke up in the morning. At school, when her teacher droned on, and some of the students nodded off, she just got restless instead. So, it didn't alarm her much to see her bedside clock display 1:00, 3:00, 5:00 and 7:00 each night.

Until the night when she didn't sleep at all.

And the night after that.

Okay, maybe he'll jump at a chance to make a medical case history out of me. If he figures out what's wrong with me, then he deserves a Nobel Prize. This isn't normal.

"Look, I *can't* sleep," she cut in. "I *don't* sleep. I stay up all night staring at the ceiling. I haven't slept for, like…" She caught herself again, then forced the words from her mouth. "Four months. Straight."

Dr. Zane had leaned forward as she said this, his brow furrowing, but now he sat back, his face clearing like the end of a storm. "Oh, you're worrying too much."

Her voice rose. "I already said I'm not! There's something wrong with me. Test me!"

"Aurora, I don't need to examine you to know that you're sleeping," said Dr. Zane. "If you went more than ten days without sleep, you'd be dead. You're sleeping. You just don't remember sleeping. Now, about those relaxation exercises…"

She slumped back in her seat. *Maybe I dream about the clock showing me 3:00 a.m. Maybe I dream of listening to the BBC World Service because I've heard all the other podcasts several times. Or maybe I'm dead and haven't realized it yet.*

Funny, though. I would have thought the dead got lots of sleep.

⚘

Aurora blinked away the memory and closed her eyes.

You've done this before. Just close your eyes and take deep, slow breaths. Cleansing air in. Stressed air out. Let the day's jumbled thoughts slip beneath the waters of silence, if not sleep.

The clock display flipped to 3:20 a.m.

After two hours of deep breathing and thoughtful silence, courtesy of Dr. Zane, Aurora looked over at her clock radio and saw the display flip to 5:25. Outside her window, she saw the first glimmer of dawn. The drapes twisted in a cool breeze and brought the smell of rain. Somewhere, with the sound of distant rolling kegs, thunder rumbled.

Aurora rolled out of her bed and padded to the bathroom. In front of the mirror, she dragged a comb through her bed-matted hair and stared at her reflection. Other than some troublesome pimples, and that little snub nose she hated, the face staring back at her was that of a typical, mildly pretty, teenaged girl. She didn't even have rings under her eyes.

"Not bad for a dead girl," she muttered.

I'm not dead, am I? I'm just weird. A great medical mystery. I'd spend the rest of my life in sleep laboratories if I could get any doctor to believe, for one second, that I've been wide awake, now, for three years and count—

Aurora froze with her hand halfway to the knob of her bedroom door.

I did sleep. In the car, when Mom played that tape on me. It was the first time I can recall sleeping since I got my period.

Her hand fell to her side.

"Mom, what did you do to me?"

And why?

In the diner, Aurora got the coffee ready and laid out the cutlery. In the kitchen, Matron turned on the toasting machine—a ludicrously large device that could toast bread for a restaurant four times the diner's size and eight times the diner's clientele—and the diner filled with the smell of roasting crumbs. Matron turned on the grill and scraped it down.

Aurora watched as the dawn fought to brighten against a line of dark clouds along the horizon. As she worked, she caught flashes of lightning out of the corner of her eye. Moments later, the sound of distant thunder rolled across the fields.

A thunderstorm. Was that good for the crops this time of year? Her country-girl self hadn't needed to ask, but her real self hadn't a clue.

Gravel crunched outside as the first pick-up pulled up. The door jangled. Ike Henderson slid into the booth seat. "Hey, Aurora."

"Hello, Mr. Henderson," said Aurora. "You by your-self?"

Ike nodded. "Molly and Britney will be along for dinner, but I got work to do."

"Farm work?"

"What do you think?" He grinned at her.

Aurora winced. It had sounded lame, but she couldn't think of anything else to say. The memories of her city girl upbringing had robbed her of country small talk. She poured a cup of coffee and set the mug in front of him. As he nodded his thanks, their eyes met.

Ike drives his tractor, turning the black soil over. The field behind the plow turns to long, straight furrows. The ground sprouts green, then yellow, as the stalks rise up. He glances behind him, and smiles.

On the horizon, a thunderstorm rumbles. Somewhere, a crow caws.

As she snapped out of the dream, the crow's caw echoing in her ears, Mr. Henderson turned to look at the cloudy horizon beyond the window. "Odd storm, coming in from the east like that," he said. "It's like it's rolling in backwards."

She frowned. "What do you mean?" But there was another crunch of gravel outside, and a car door slammed.

The storm brewed as the day drew on, and people came and left. The clouds turned into mountain peaks under the noonday sun. Aurora couldn't stop herself from taking quick glances at it as she polished the table tops or served up the meals through lunch.

After two there were no more tables to polish, no more cutlery to rearrange. The diner was empty. Polk and Matron came out of the kitchen. Polk grabbed some ketchup bottles to be refilled while Matron flipped between the TV channels, looking for news.

Aurora tossed her towel over her shoulder and sat down at the counter near them. "Slow day," she said.

Polk shrugged. "It happens. Sometimes people decide to make their own lunches. Shocking, I know. It should be banned—"

From her stool, Aurora kicked him in the shin.

"Ow!" He whined theatrically. "Matron!"

"Now, now," said Matron, giving up and leaving the TV muted on a trashy reality show. "None of that." She plopped down a deck of cards.

"No thanks," said Aurora. "I've got a book to read." She turned towards the diner's exit.

The door jangled as she stepped outside. The gravel crunched underfoot.

Outside, halfway to the door to the apartment, Aurora stopped. She did a slow turn, scanning the whole flat landscape and listening hard to the sounds around her. Despite the storm clouds in the distance, the sun baked the back of her neck.

No cars passed on the roadway outside the diner. No kids shouted on the rusting playground swings on the corner. Starlings chirped from the tassels, but the houses of Cooper's Corners stood silent.

What am I doing here? We're out in the middle of nowhere. Mom had objected to that, when she'd called Matron, and I can see why. You'd think that if you were going to hide someone, it would be among other people. But here, in this driveway, with only the sounds of nature for company, I could imagine that all of the people had gone, and that me, Polk and Matron were the only humans left alive—alive and alone facing...what?

From the eastern horizon came the sound of distant thunder. Aurora shivered despite the summer heat.

She went into the back apartment and grabbed her book from the bedside table. Then, as she left her bedroom, she paused beside Matron's bedroom door. She'd promised herself, back when Mom had proposed bringing her here, that she'd get Matron's secret out of her, but now that she stood on the threshold of violating the woman's privacy, Aurora hesitated.

This is the woman who has cared for me all my life—okay, the past three years. She isn't one to show much affection, but she isn't all bristles and snide remarks, either. She encouraged me to go to the country social when I was sure it would do nothing but leave me holding up a wall. And I had fun, with Polk. No, Matron wasn't Mom, but she's been…okay.

And I intend to repay this by snooping around her bedroom?

But then again, people have been playing with my memories, haven't they? Blocking me from seeing them. And Matron had to be in on that.

Aurora twisted the doorknob with more vigour than she'd intended. The door swung open, and she had to catch it before it banged against the wall.

The bedroom was as neat as the rest of Matron's house and restaurant. White curtains were drawn against the window. The bed was made with white sheets and hospital corners. The closet door was closed, and the dresser was bare, save for a handheld mirror. A single shelf held a dozen cookbooks. Beneath it on the floor was a wooden chest.

It was neat. Sensible. Just like Matron. But Aurora frowned. It was more than sensible: it was without personality. This was a room withholding comment on its occupant.

Except for the wooden chest. It looked like a toy chest that might hold dress-up clothes. Aurora came forward for a closer look. It was unlocked. She opened the lid and peered in.

The box was full of old, childish junk. Aurora pulled out a raggedy doll, a bundle of ancient lollipops, a couple of building blocks, and a large book. *What were these, keepsakes? It's like an emergency kit for someone who rescues children.*

The book had no title. It was thick and had a picture of mountains on the cover. She opened it.

"Sally flies over mountains. She reaches down and touches a peak. The snow crumbles on her fingertips…"

Aurora flipped through the pages, caught images dark and light, but nothing that interested her. She put the book back in the chest and closed the lid, disappointed. It had been a fruitless search, and now Matron and Polk were going to be wondering where she was. She hurried downstairs.

On the horizon, a sun-bleached farmhouse disappeared behind a veil of rain.

Back in the diner, she sat at the counter, seats away from Matron and Polk. She kept her nose in her book, turning pages only when she remembered to, and thought of her next move.

At four, Matron stood up from the card game. "Let's get ready for dinner hour."

Before long, the gravel outside scrunched and the shop bell jangled as the usual crowd trickled in. Britney bolted through the door, followed by her mother. She ran up to Aurora, flung her arms around Aurora's legs and gave her a big hug before rushing to her seat. Aurora watched her go with a raised eyebrow, but she smiled.

The Hobsons arrived a few minutes later, followed by the Pankiws, then the farmhands from the fields. Soon the place was chattering, and Aurora was working the tables. Hamburgers and fries. A Hungry Man (four eggs, four bacon, four sausages, ham and a coronary). Some of Matron's pot pie. Aurora carried the plates to their tables as the orders arrived.

When there was nothing left for Aurora to do but refill the coffee, she jabbed the buttons on the remote—the regulars liked to ignore the six o'clock news while they ate their meals—but she couldn't find a signal. She gave up when she spied Britney finishing the last of her burger and pushing the tomato to the side of her plate with the end of her knife, eyes narrowing in disdain. Aurora then began tallying orders on the cash register and delivering them one by one to the tables.

"So, how was everything?" Aurora asked the Hobsons as she scribbled on her notepad. She ripped off the slip and held it out. Then she stared a long moment, wondering why she was holding a bill out to an empty booth.

She looked to her left, then her right. The Hobsons should have been in front of her, but they weren't, and they weren't at any of the other tables either.

Aurora crumpled the bill and darted for the kitchen. Matron looked up as she burst in.

"The Hobsons!" said Aurora. "They skipped out without paying!"

"What are you talking about?" said Matron.

"What do you mean, what am I talking about?" Aurora waved her arms. "Hobson family. They had one roast beef and one Eggs Benedict plus a whole lot of coffee and two slices of pie. $29.95, not including taxes and tip! I wrote up their bill, but they left before I could hand it to them!" Then she realized that Matron was frowning at her, rather than at the news. "What?"

"I never made up an order for Eggs Benedict," said Matron.

Aurora gawped at her. "But...I took their order!"

Matron shrugged and turned back to the grill. "Well, if you did, you didn't hand it to me. Maybe that's why they left without paying."

"But I *served* them! You cooked it up!" Aurora stared at Matron. "You've got to remember!"

Matron clucked her tongue. "You're imagining things, girl. I know what I served up to my customers today, and Eggs Benedict wasn't on that list. Maybe you were remembering yesterday? Maybe one of yesterday's bills got mixed up in your hands?"

Aurora bit her lip. Then she took a deep breath. "Yeah," she said. "Must be."

She turned on her heel and strode out of the kitchen.

Aurora looked up and down the diner. She could hear distant thunder rolling outside over the sounds of people eating their dinner. Save for the Hobsons, everybody else was here. Ike Henderson got up from the table, stretched, and ambled toward the washroom.

"Hey, Aurora!" shouted Jake, a gawky farmhand sitting with his friends in a booth.

Without thinking, Aurora looked at him. Their eyes met.

*The bikini is very, very small, and Aurora is very, very...
bouncy as she races down the sand, giggling and...*

Aurora gave him a look that could melt cast iron.
"What?" she bellowed, making the diners around her
jump.

The farmhand went pale. His friends at the table started
to snicker. He gulped and held up an empty glass. "Um...
more water...please?"

The sky darkens. There is a flash of lightning.

Aurora looked away, ashamed of herself. It wasn't like
he could control his dreams or know that she wanted him
to. She didn't need to strike him down with lightning,
tempting though that was. "Sure," she muttered, and went
behind the counter.

As she pulled a glass from the rack and filled it from
the tap, she frowned. The thunder and lightning hadn't
been something she had done. It was a part of Jake's
dream. But thunder and lightning on the beach? Why
would the storm invade his dream like that?

And why does "invade" sound so right?

She jumped as the water overflowed the glass and ran
over her hand. She shut off the tap, poured a little out,
then marched over to Jake's table and plunked the glass in
front of him. "Thanks," he said. Then she looked up.

The booth was empty.

Aurora stepped back, tripped on her feet and fell, catching herself on the stools by the counter.

The diner silenced. She felt nearly a dozen pairs of eyes
stare at her, and her cheeks reddened. She pushed herself
back to her feet. "It's okay," she said. "I'm okay."

44

But it wasn't okay. The ripple of conversation was quieter than it had been a couple of minutes ago. She was seeing more empty vinyl where there should have been people. There'd been no sound of the bell on the doorjamb jingling, she was sure of it. No one had left the restaurant in the last ten minutes, and yet the noise level had gone steadily down.

At the far end of the diner, Aurora saw Mr. Radwanski pull his wallet from his pocket. She grabbed up his bill. Keeping him in sight as she walked up to him, she looked down at the last moment to total his bill. She tore off the slip. "So, was everything okay?"

She stared at an empty booth.

"Aurora? Are you all right?"

The diners were staring at her again. The remains of them, anyway. And in the kitchen, Matron's grill sizzled like nothing was wrong. Thunder rumbled.

She tried to slow her thumping heart. Failed. This was getting worse.

Then her eyes shot back to Mrs. Henderson and Britney. What was wrong with this picture? Then she remembered. Mr. Henderson still hadn't come back from the bathroom.

Ignoring the looks of the remaining customers, Aurora barged into the men's room. At the urinal, Polk yelped and zipped himself up. "Hey!"

There was only one sink, one urinal and one stall with a toilet. Aurora crouched and peered beneath the barrier. There were no feet in front of the toilet. "Where's Mr. Henderson?"

Polk cast the damp towels into the waste bin. "What are you talking about?"

She straightened up. "Ike Henderson! You know who he is, don't you?"

"Of course I do!" He frowned at her. "Aurora, what's going on?"

"Did he come in here?"

"No."

"What?" Aurora scanned the walls for hidden doorways, hatches. "He came in here! I saw him go in here! Didn't you see him?" She turned this way and that in the middle of the small room. "Mr. Henderson! Where are you?"

Polk caught her by the shoulders and held on as she struggled. "Calm down!"

She slapped his hands away. "Don't you tell me to calm down! Either Ike Henderson was here and he disappeared, or I'm losing my mind! So, which is it, huh?"

"Um..." He swallowed. "Which do you want it to be?"

She turned away with an exasperated yowl and burst out of the washroom...

...into an empty diner.

The grill was silent. Behind her, the door to the empty men's room swung on its hinges.

The jangling of the bell caught her attention and Aurora looked at the door. Mrs. Henderson held it open for her daughter. They were leaving. Alone. The last customers of the night. The door swung shut behind them.

Aurora charged the length of the diner. "Mrs. Henderson! Wait!"

She ran out the door and looked around wildly. In the

dying light of the sun, she saw a young girl standing with her doll in the middle of the road.

"Britney!" Aurora cried. The girl turned, her doll hanging by her side. Aurora ran onto the road and pulled Britney to the shoulder.

Aurora knelt in front of Britney and looked her in the eye.

Britney swings in Aurora's arms, twirling around the wheat stalks, laughing. Mr. Scaly is safely locked inside his pet carrier. The sun shines and the birds sing.

The sky darkens.

Over Aurora's shoulder, clouds appear, solidifying into a thousand black shapes, flapping closer.

Aurora blinked. Britney stared back, lost but strangely calm.

"He's coming for you," said the girl.

"What?!" Aurora shook the strange vision out of her head. "What were you doing out here?" She tried to keep the edge out of her voice. "You can't just stand in the middle of the road like that. What would your parents think?"

Britney blinked. "Not here," she said distantly. "Mom. Dad. Not here."

Aurora swallowed. *This is getting worse. Scratch that. It had passed worse and was well on its way to catastrophic.* "Come inside, Britney. C'mon, let's get some ice cream."

Britney looked up at her with wide eyes. "Chock-lit?"

Aurora smiled. "Of course."

As she stepped towards the diner, she felt Britney's hand slip from her fingers. Aurora turned. She was alone on the gravel driveway. Around her, the wind sighed in the grain.

"Britney?" she shouted. "Britney!"

Britney's doll lay sprawled on the gravel. Aurora picked it up and clasped it to her shoulder. Thunder rumbled.

Aurora turned. The clouds were almost upon her.

She drew breath for a scream, but the words caught in her throat as a crow cawed. Aurora's gaze shot round and then she saw it, perched atop the power pole where the gravel drive met the wheat field. *One crow for sorrow*, she thought.

"Aaa! Aaa!" said the crow, a sound like a rusty gate. Then, "Aaa! Roa! Raa!"

Aurora blinked.

The crow stretched its wings and kicked off its perch, coasting down into the wheat field and perching on a combine. It tucked its wings in and looked back at her, focusing on her with one eye, then the other. It cawed again: "Aaa! Roa! Raa!"

Aurora shouted. "Who are you? What do you want? What did you do to all the people?"

"Aaa! Roa! Raa!"

My name?

"I know who I am! Tell me something I *don't* know!"

"He! He!" the crow cawed. Then, "He! Comes!"

Movement caught her eye, and she looked up at the billowing clouds. Crows were flying in from every direction, hovering in the air in front of her, forming like a cloud of starlings, then like smoke. As Aurora watched, the cloud pulled itself into shape. She could make out the beginnings of a head, two arms, hands outstretched in a gesture like longing—

"Aurora! Wake up!" Matron shouted.

Aurora whirled around and stared down the barrel of a Browning rifle. She hit the muddy dirt as Matron fired over her head. The crows scattered, crying murder—

Aurora snapped awake, gasping and dripping.

Matron pulled her up with one hand, the other holding her rifle.

"Oh, thank God," gasped Aurora. "It was only a dream."

Matron looked pale. "You're awake. And now you need to run."

"What?" She blinked. "And since when do you own a rifle?" *Wait a minute, what was the rifle still doing here? Wasn't it part of the dream?*

"Look around you, girl!"

Aurora turned and immediately wished she hadn't. The billowing, twisting grey clouds were still there. They had turned black and feathery, and they were descending. Shingles were blowing off the houses in Cooper's Corners. Somewhere, a window smashed.

"Where is everybody?" Aurora yelled.

"They're sheltering," Matron shouted. "Waiting for the storm to pass, but it won't. Not while you're here." She drew back the pump of the rifle, a classic *click-click*. Then she came closer and looked Aurora in the eye. "You know, don't you? Don't try to deny it, girl, I can see it in your eyes. After all the trouble your mom went through to put you to sleep, you woke up. I thought you might. You were always a stubborn child."

So many things that she wanted to say crowded into Aurora's mouth, and she spluttered.

Matron hefted the weapon onto her shoulder. "Maybe it's for the best. He's coming for you. It's best you be wide awake when you run."

"Run from who? Who's coming for me?"

"No time!"

"Where should I go?"

"Saskatoon." Matron shoved a piece of paper at her, along with a set of car keys. "I've written down the address. I can't keep you safe anymore, so you need to get back to her."

"Back to who? What are you talking about?" Aurora wanted to scream and cry and shake Matron to make her explain. "Since when am I allowed to drive?"

"No more questions!" Matron yelled over the rising rumble of the wind and the cry of crows. "Just go! Go now! You can't let him take you, girl! It will be disaster if he does!"

Aurora looked up at the spiralling clouds again. She froze.

"Run, you idiot!" Matron yelled. "Run!"

Aurora ran, mud squelching and gravel crunching. Matron's battered brown Chevy came into view. Slipping and skidding, she caught herself with one hand on the car roof and fumbled with the door handle. It was unlocked and opened suddenly, knocking her hand, sending the keys to the gravel. Aurora twisted to pick them up and fell over into a puddle.

The light went out of the sky.

Aurora grabbed the keys, dove into the car and slammed the door. The car shook in the buffeting winds. Without thinking, she pulled on her seat belt and checked the rear-view mirror. She cried out.

The crows had descended on Matron like a funnel cloud. Matron brought up her rifle and sighted along the barrel.

Aurora turned the key in the ignition, just like Matron had taught her. The station wagon sputtered to life, and she danced on the clutch. Gears creaked as she shoved it into first gear. Wheels spinning, gravel spraying, she man-handled the car onto the road. Second gear and the car picked up speed. Third gear. Go.

Behind her, she heard the rifle blast, and the murder of crows.

CHAPTER THREE:
PAST THE HUNDREDTH MERIDIAN

THE FIRST DREAM AURORA READ BELONGED TO her best friend, Anne.

It was at school, grade six, and Aurora was just hanging up her new spring jacket. Standing back to appreciate the dark denim, she bumped into Anne.

Anne caught her arm. "Hey! Watch it!" But not unkindly. "*Nice* jacket."

"Thanks!" Aurora beamed. "Mom bought it for me on the weekend. We went out to that new place out by the power centre. Isn't it cool?"

"Yeah, I saw you wearing it at the mall yesterday," said Anne.

"Oh," said Aurora. "Why didn't you say hello?"

"I was just heading out," said Anne quickly. She shrugged off her brown polyester coat and tossed it onto a hook. It flopped on the floor instead. Anne sighed and bent to pick it up.

As she placed it back on its hook, a slab of a boy shouldered her aside. He threw her coat on the floor.

"Hey!" Anne shouted. She caught her breath when she saw who the boy was. Aurora froze. Roger had already

won two fights that the teachers knew about, and more
that they didn't. If that wasn't enough, Roger's friend and
henchman, Jack, was right behind him.

Roger sneered. "Get your own hook." He hung his
parka from the disputed hook with sausage-like fingers.

Anne's breathing quickened. "C'mon, there's a free
hook right over there!" She reached for her coat.

Roger pushed her back. "Your trashy old Goodwill
coat belongs in the garbage, anyway." He leered at them.
"Unless you wanna make something of it."

There was an adult throat-clearing. Miss Daultry leaned
in from the classroom. "Is there a problem here?"

Aurora opened her mouth, but Roger caught her eye.
He and Jack stuck their hands in their pockets and stood,
waiting.

Anne glared at the floor. "No, Miss Daultry. Everything's okay."

The teacher frowned over her glasses, then turned
away. Grinning, Roger and Jack followed her into the classroom. Anne thumped the wall.

"It's okay," said Aurora. "Share my hook."

Anne forced a smile. "Thanks," she said. Without
meaning to, Aurora looked into her friend's brown eyes.

*Anne snatches Aurora's denim jacket and runs across
the classroom, laughing, impervious to Aurora's pleas. She
flings it out the window into a lake that has materialized in
place of the schoolyard.*

Aurora shook her head and looked around. Her jacket
was still on its hook, and the classroom windows were
closed. Anne had turned away and was slinking out of the

cloakroom to take her seat as Miss Daultry called the class
to order.

"Aurora," Miss Daultry called. "Won't you grace us with
your presence?"

The rest of the class giggled, but Aurora was too distracted to be embarrassed as she slouched out of the cloakroom to take her seat beside her friend.

Aurora read her second dream before recess. As the
rest of the class filed out, Miss Daultry pulled her aside.
"Is anything the matter, Aurora? You've been distracted all
morning."

Aurora kept her gaze on the lower half of the teacher's
face. "Nothing's wrong."

"You're sure?" Her teacher gave her an encouraging
smile. "You can always talk to me."

Aurora looked into Miss Daultry's eyes.

*Miss Daultry kicks back at her desk and pulls out a good
book. Around her, the classroom stands empty, the windows
white with snow. School is cancelled. No children today.
Miss Daultry inspects a box of chocolates, picks one, and
settles in to read.*

Aurora dropped her gaze to the floor. "I'm sure. Nothing's the matter. Can I go?"

Miss Daultry's eyes narrowed a moment. Then she patted Aurora on the shoulder. "Okay. Get going."

At recess, Aurora played hide and seek and agreed to be
'it.' As the other kids ran away, Aurora hunted them down
methodically, pouncing on each boy or girl, and looking
them in the eye. Visions flooded her.

...I did it! I scored the winning goal!...

...I get to meet Santa! And they told me he wasn't real!...
Jack glared at Aurora. "What are you smiling at?"

"Nothing." Aurora moved on.

...Yes! I just punched Roger's face in!...

As she searched from person to person, a certainty rose in her from somewhere deep inside about what these were: these were dreams. These were personal. These were wants, hopes, remembrances, these were...

...No. The planes are back. The sirens are wailing. The bombs are falling again...

Albijana grimaced as Aurora flinched in horror. "Stop staring, Aurora! You're weird!" She pushed past Aurora and ran for home base.

Finally, at the end of the day, Aurora fumbled on her coat in the cloakroom, lost in thought.

"Hey," said Anne. Aurora jumped.

"You've been quiet all day," said Anne as she yanked on her too-small, salt-stained, balding fur-lined boots.

"Why do you want to throw my coat into a lake?" said Aurora.

Anne froze. She looked up and laughed nervously. "What are you talking—?"

Aurora looked into Anne's eyes.

Anne laughs. Aurora's denim jacket sails out the window and lands with a splash before sinking without a trace. Aurora sobs, standing in Anne's ratty clothes.

Aurora stepped back. "You're jealous!"

Anne gaped at her. "No—what? Aurora!"

"You want to grab my jacket and toss it into a lake. You hate that I have a new jacket and you've got an old one!"

Anne gasped. "How did you—?" Then her eyes flashed. "You read my diary!"

Aurora flinched. "I didn't! I—" She froze. How could she explain how she knew? But she didn't feel like she should be the one to be ashamed, here. "It doesn't matter. You've been jealous the whole time we've been together, thinking all those things behind my back."

"You think I meant it?" Anne drew a shaky breath. "Yeah, sure, I want the things you have, but that doesn't mean I don't like you. It was just a dream. I still liked you. Until now! You traitor!"

Anne stormed out of the cloakroom. She came storming back to pick up her remaining boot and stormed out again. This time she was choking back sobs.

Aurora watched her go, blinking back her own tears.

The rain stopped a few miles down the road, but black clouds loomed in the rear-view mirror. Aurora drove through the sunset and into the night – longer than all her previous drives she'd taken. She passed a sign which said SASKATOON: 390 KM.

Soon the only sound was the hum of the engine as her headlights turned the road into a small pool in the middle of a rolling void. More signposts appeared, slowly counting down the distance. Eventually, she ignored them and focused on the black ribbon of road ahead of her. She ignored the stars, ignored the horizon as it began to brighten. Finally, as she topped a hill and drove into sunshine, she had to blink.

She tried not to remember Matron standing with her gun raised as the feathery clouds descended.

She sobbed and hated herself for it. Crying was what little kids did. She was a teenager. On her own. In a car she could barely drive, fleeing from some monster who could attack in dreams and in the waking world at the same time. Heading southeast to Saskatoon to meet... who? There was no one she could turn to—

Someone breathed behind her. A hand clasped her shoulder. "Hey—"

Aurora screamed.

From the back seat, Polk screamed.

"What are you doing here?" Aurora shouted.

He looked past her and his eyes widened. "Watch the road!"

She turned around, squeaked, and twisted the wheel. The car skidded on the edge of the ditch, then eased back onto the road. Aurora took a deep breath. "What are you doing here?" She grabbed a quick look back before facing the road ahead.

"I needed a nap," he said, "so I snuck out to Matron's car, lay down and fell asleep. She never thinks to look for me here. Have I been asleep long?"

Aurora kept her eyes forward. Before them, on their left, the sun climbed farther up into the sky. "A while."

Polk squirmed over the top of the passenger seat and slithered down beside her. He gave her a goofy grin. Then he frowned. "You're not old enough to drive."

"Give me a break! I'm almost sixteen! I've got a learner's permit."

Polk raised his eyebrows.

"Okay, I could *get* my learner's permit, if I'd spent the time to actually get one. But I'm old enough to drive!"

"Okay." Polk settled into his seat. He shielded his eyes against the sun, then folded down the sunshield. The grogginess in his gaze disappeared, as though a sudden cold wind had cleared his mind. He blinked into the sunshine. "Wait a minute. Is that... sunrise?"

"Yes."

"I slept the night?"

"Yes."

"Have we been driving all night?"

"Yes."

"Matron's back at the diner, right?"

Aurora choked, then swallowed. "Y-yes," she said at last. *I hope so anyhow.*

Polk looked from her to the road ahead and back again.

"We've been driving all night?" he said again.

"Yes."

"Why were we driving all night?"

Aurora didn't answer.

"Does Matron know you took her car?"

She nodded.

"Aurora? What's going on?"

She thumped the wheel with her forehead. The car swerved. "Just shut up! Shut up! Shut the hell up!"

Polk clutched the armrest. He hurriedly did up his seat belt. "Aurora, calm down."

"Calm?" Aurora rounded on him. Polk cringed in his seat, but she didn't care. "Calm? How do you expect me to be calm? I saw the whole village disappear before my eyes! Crows talked to me! Then I found it was just a dream, but I woke up into a storm and the crows were still there and they attacked Matron! She could be dead for all we know, and you expect me to be calm? I can't be calm! I'm exhausted and scared and confused, and I don't know what to do except drive! So that's what I'm doing! *Okay?*"

"Aurora," Polk said softly. "Stop the car."

"What?"

"Just... pull over and stop the car." He sounded ultra-calm. "Please?"

They pulled onto the shoulder. The car tilted, perched at the edge of the ditch. When they were stopped, Polk reached over and moved the gearshift to park. Aurora stared at the wheel.

Polk gripped the door handle, then turned to her. "Kill the engine. Let's stretch our legs."

"What for?"

He gave her a smile. "Trust me." He opened the door and slid out, disappearing into the ditch with a yelp. He popped up seconds later, grinned at her, and trudged to the back of the car.

Aurora made to kill the engine then realized that she couldn't uncurl her fingers from the steering wheel. She pulled back hard until her fingers slipped from the vinyl and came away, curled into claws. She flattened them on her lap and flexed them, wincing as they uncramped. She shook them to get some life back into them.

She turned off the ignition and left the car keys on the seat as she hauled herself outside. She came around back to where Polk leaned against the trunk. They stood on the broken paved shoulder, grassy where it met the drainage ditch. Aurora stared out at the rippling fields. A chill wind, left over from the night, touched her cheeks and plucked at her hair.

Polk just stood there. She looked at him. "You waiting for something?"

He waved a hand at the fields of grass and flower stretching on forever. "Just take a minute. Breathe. Talk. Scream. Cry. Whatever comes to you. You'll know what to do. You just need to let it out. It's safer to do it out here instead of behind the wheel."

"When did you get all Zen?"

He gave her a teasing smile. "Hey, I have hidden depths."

She turned and walked away. Asphalt crunched as she trudged along the shoulder up a low rise. When she reached the top, she looked around. The fields dipped away, a sea of yellow-green waves breaking against posts and barbed wire fences. The wind made a sound like surf. Blackbirds tweedled, but there were no crows.

You know what to do, she thought. *Just let it out.*

She took a deep breath and howled.

Her voice rang in her ears, powered by all the rage and confusion and fear that had built up over the past day and a half. She screamed one long note that bent her over as the air left her lungs. The scream stopped. She straightened up, pulling in air, arching her back.

"Mom! Where are you?" she hollered. "How could you leave me like this? How could you?"

She hollered until she was bent almost double again, breathing heavily, her hands on her knees. Quiet again. The wind rushed through the tassels like waves on the ocean. The only other sound was Polk scuffing the pavement with his toe.

Aurora straightened up. Her cheeks were wet, but she wiped them dry on her sleeve and cleared her nose with a sniff. She stood a moment, drinking in the isolation, the endless blue sky, the yellow fields, and brought her breathing under control. Cleansing breath in, stressed air out. Cleansing breath in. Hold it. Then let it out.

She set her jaw. There were no answers blowing in the wind. She was on her own, so she wasn't going to waste her time curled up in a ball and weeping.

She strode back to the car. Polk stood leaning on it. She leaned beside him and looked ahead. "Thanks."

"You're welcome. So, what's going on?"

She looked away in disgust. "You wouldn't believe me."

He grinned. "You have the car. You have the keys, and it's a long walk back to Matron's. I don't think it would be wise for me to disbelieve you."

She just looked at him.

His grin vanished. "What happened?"

Aurora's hands clenched into fists. She banged the trunk. How could she even begin to explain? But she had to tell someone.

"I—" She stopped, then started again. "I had a dream. I dreamed that we were working the diner, like we always do, and the dinner crowd came in, but they started to disappear one by one. Everyone I knew in Cooper's Corners

vanished, leaving me out in the open, all alone when…
something…came for me.”

He turned to her, his expression sympathetic. “That’s a
horrible nightmare, but—”

“Polk, I didn’t dream that last night, or the night
before. I dreamed it yesterday afternoon!”

“That’s impossible.”

“No. It happened. Polk, what did I do yesterday? Did I
talk to you after the dinner crowd came in? What?”

“No.” He shrugged. “You took orders, served them
up. You were a little distant, though. Like you were sleepwalk—” He stopped and stared at her, eyes wide. “You’re
serious? You were asleep then?”

“Yes.”

“You didn’t spill a drop of coffee—”

“That’s not important! Polk, it wasn’t normal. Something attacked me. And in my dream, I walked out to the
field behind the diner. That’s when Matron found me and
woke me up. Except when I woke up, the dream was still
around me.”

He straightened up. “What do you mean?”

“There was a storm in my dream,” said Aurora. “And
when I woke up, it was all around me. I saw twisting
clouds, and I heard windows breaking.”

“My God. Was everybody okay?”

“I don’t know. Matron made me get in her car and go.
She said the storm would follow me, and everybody else
would be safe. Then the crows attacked her, and—”

The colour drained from Polk’s face. “Is...she okay?”

Aurora drew a shaky breath. “I don’t know.”

They stood in silence on either side of the parked car, staring at each other. "This is silly," said Polk. "Running away because of some dream you had. If Matron's hurt, or if the town…We should go back. It's not like the storm's actually following—"

A rumble echoed across the fields, like barrels rolling across a stage. Aurora and Polk looked north, back the way they'd come. The sky was still blue, but the horizon was dark and growing darker.

They looked back at each other. The breeze plucked at their hair.

"So, where do we go?" said Polk at last.

"South," said Aurora.

"Why south?"

"That's the way the car's facing."

"Fair enough." Polk straightened up and came around to the driver's side. "Get in. My turn to drive."

Aurora leaned on the driver's side door. "I'm driving."

He pulled at the handle. "You're not legal."

She slapped his hand away. "I want to drive."

And she did too, she realized. It was the one thing she could control in this world gone haywire. There was no way she was going to fidget in the passenger seat.

"Hey!" Polk slapped her hand back.

Aurora shoved him.

He staggered back, then came forward angrily. Aurora raised her fists.

Polk threw up his hands. "Fine! Just don't crash." He stomped to the passenger door. Aurora allowed herself a small smile as she slipped behind the wheel.

"Matron gave me an address," she added as she started the engine. "Somebody in Saskatoon who could help me, she said. It's as good a place as any." The car drove off with a spray of gravel.

"Saskatoon," Polk murmured.

They passed a sign: SASKATOON, 300 KM. Polk twisted in his seat to stare at it as it passed. He looked back at Aurora. "Something's wrong."

Aurora laughed. "You just figured that out?"

His expression didn't change. "Did you really drive all night?"

"Yeah."

"Did you stop at all?"

"No."

"Not even to go to the bathroom?"

"No."

"You tired?"

"No."

"You hungry?"

"No."

"You have to go to the bathroom?"

"No."

"Look: did you, or did you not, drive away yesterday evening at top speed?"

Aurora flushed, thinking of how she'd abandoned Matron. "What are you getting at?"

"You picked the road to Saskatoon, right? You just drove straight?"

"Yes!" Her knuckles whitened on the wheel. "Polk—"

"Saskatchewan's big, but it's not *that* big, and we're not

that far north. It's a five-hour drive, tops, between Cooper's Corners and Saskatoon. If you left soon after I went to sleep, and it's sunrise now, you're looking at, what, eight hours? Ten? You should be well on your way to Billings, Montana, by now."

"Polk, just be quiet and let me drive." New nerves twisted in her stomach. She *didn't* know how big Saskatchewan was. The lack of knowledge reminded her that she wasn't a local and that her years here had been a lie.

They passed another signpost: SASKATOON: 300 KM

Aurora and Polk exchanged glances. They drove on in silence for a few minutes.

The next signpost read: SASKATOON: 300 KM

Polk twisted to look at the sign as it passed. "Okay... were you...sleep-driving, maybe?"

"We're not driving in circles." Aurora scanned the dashboard.

"Except that I'd have to be sleep-driving too. How does *that* work?"

The next sign said: SASKATOON: 300 KM

It's like in a dream, Aurora thought, *where you keep running as fast as you can but don't get anywhere. Very like a dream.*

So, how do I wake myself up?

She glanced at her wrist, then gave it a quick pinch. She looked at the road ahead. Nothing happened. She pinched harder. She looked ahead. The sign appeared on the horizon again. Then she took a deep breath and put all of her strength into her thumb and forefinger.

"Ow!"

The world shuddered.

The car swerved. Where the road had been straight, now they were rushing headlong towards a curve. The sun was higher in the sky. They passed an abandoned farmhouse they hadn't seen before.

"What the hell?" said Polk.

"We're out of the dream," said Aurora. "I think."

"How can you tell?"

Another sign appeared over the crest of a hill. Polk and Aurora held their breath.

SASKATOON: 290 KM

"Okay," said Polk. "Let's find someplace to stop and get some breakfast."

"What?" Aurora gaped at him. "After all that, you want to stop?"

"Look, we can't just drive on without stopping. We need to eat. And if we don't want to stink up Matron's car, we'll need to use the bathroom."

"If you need to go to the bathroom so bad, you can go in the bushes. You can forget about food. I left my purse back at Matron's. There's no money."

"I got money."

She glanced at him. "How much?"

He looked up at the ceiling, calculating. "About a thousand dollars."

"What?!" The car swerved.

"Would you *please* get a handle on your reactions?" said Polk. "I swear, someone says boo, and we'll end up upside-down in the ditch."

"Sorry," said Aurora crossly. "But, how—?"

He shrugged. "It just sort of...accumulated. The nearest

bank's fifty miles away, after all. Though I think we may have passed it sometime in the night."

She looked ahead. "I see."

"So, can we stop?"

"I said I wasn't hungry!"

"And *I* called you a liar. Besides, we have to stop: the empty tank alert just came on."

Aurora looked at the dashboard. A red gas tank icon shone back at her. She swore under her breath.

They passed a signpost for the next small town, but Aurora didn't catch its name.

Minutes later, they crested a hill and Aurora looked down on a settlement consisting of a single shuttered house and a general store. The store was built of wood and painted red. Gas pumps squatted on the gravel driveway. In the distance, a grain tower stood guarded by rail cars.

"Ah, civilization," Polk breathed. He chuckled. "Well, almost. No Tim Horton's."

"Huh," said Aurora. There was something about this that didn't feel right. But she caught sight of the low gas indicator again and applied the brakes. They coasted off the road and stopped in front of the gas pumps. They had dials for numbers instead of a digital display. Aurora wondered if she should look for a hand crank.

A tall, lanky figure unfolded himself from a battered chair. He stood by the front door of the store and watched without any sign of surprise as they pulled up. When Aurora cut the engine, she took a good look at him.

He wore a dark brown suit jacket over a white T-shirt and khaki pants and black leather shoes. His brown hair was thinning on top, and he had a small brown goatee. His moustache had been manicured into two brown lines below his nose, with curled-up ends. He gave them a thin-lipped smile, then threw his arms wide.

"Customers!" he cried. "Welcome to my store!"

Aurora stopped in her tracks. Nobody greeted customers this way unless they were desperate for business. And nobody was this desperate for business unless they hadn't had any for weeks, if not years.

The store building looked sturdy but old. The paint had faded, and there were sun-bleached boxes and other bric-a-brac stacked along the foundation. In the nearby fields, two dusty plastic bags rose and twisted over the barley, caught in an updraft.

Polk nodded at the store owner. "We're looking for gas and breakfast. Got either?"

"Both!" chimed the owner. "Come in! Fill up man and machine, why don't you?" He waved grandly at the front door.

Polk stepped forward, but Aurora caught his arm. "Is this guy for real?" she whispered.

"He doesn't have to be for real," Polk murmured. "He just has to know how to cook some steak and eggs. I'm hungry."

"You're *always* hungry."

"I'll pump. You order."

She nodded, then turned back to the store owner. "Thanks... uh..."

"Call me Salvadore." He beckoned from the threshold. "Come, let us not dally." A battered screen door slammed behind him.

Aurora followed him up the front steps. As she reached for the door, a noise made her freeze. It sounded like a baby rattle. She shrugged, yanked open the gap-riddled screen door, and entered.

The shop bell jangled. Aurora gagged, caught off guard by a sudden musty smell that washed over her. But when she looked around, the smell faded. The interior of the store shone clean and bright.

There were five aisles, numbered with signs that hung down from the ceiling. The shelves were loaded with gleaming cans and shiny plastic-wrapped packages. A display of red licorice glistened beside the cash register. Along one wall, near the entrance to the washrooms, was an ice cream stand and a soda jerk. There was a grill nearby, warm and freshly oiled, and Aurora was hit with a memory of Matron's diner. She swallowed the lump in her throat.

Sniffing the air again, all she could smell was fresh produce—apples, lettuce—and cleaning fluid. Lots of it.

"So, what shall I get you?" Salvadore tied a spotless white apron around his waist and stood behind the counter.

"Steak and eggs for Polk," said Aurora. "Sausage and eggs for me, please."

"How do you like your eggs?"

"Scrambled for Polk. Mine, over easy. We'll have toast, too."

Salvadore got two sausage rounds and a small steak

from the refrigerator and set them on the grill to sizzle. Then he grabbed four eggs, tossing each in the air before catching them and cracking them on the side of the grill.

Showy. Aurora rolled her eyes. Matron never showed off with the customers' meals. *And he's put on the eggs too quickly. They'd be done and cooling well before the steak was ready. No wonder he's starved for customers.*

As the food cooked, Salvadore turned to her. "And how about a drink? An ice cream soda, perhaps?"

Aurora had been about to order coffee, but a soda sounded good. "Yeah, sure."

"One for you and one for your boyfriend?"

"He's *not* my boyfriend."

"So, one soda or two?"

"One. Polk can order whatever he wants."

"One soda. Two straws?" Salvadore grinned at her and cast an eye out the front door where they'd left Polk with the gas.

She glanced out the screen door and saw Polk by the car. He had the pump handle in the car's gas tank and was puzzling over the unfamiliar levers.

She turned back to Salvadore. "Whatever," she said, deliberately.

Salvadore grabbed a frosted glass from the refrigerator. He began scooping out ice cream and added a dollop of syrup. "So, what brings you out here?"

Aurora looked at him without expression, but he kept smiling as he worked away. "Driving," she said at last.

"Where to?"

None of your business. "South."

He grinned at her. "Forgive me. I don't get many customers these days, and it does a number on the art of
conversation."

"So where have all the customers gone?"

He jerked his shoulders in a shrug. "You know how it
is."

"Not really."

"It's Saskatchewan, love! Not much reason to stay,
unless you like the scenery."

"So, why do you stay?"

"I like the scenery. Besides, there's still business. You
two turned up, after all."

She hadn't met a single car or truck since running away
from Matron's diner.

He handed over a frosty glass. "There you go! One ice
cream soda, *two* straws." He grinned that irritating grin
again. He was worse than Polk.

Aurora took the ice cream soda. "Thanks." She put both
straws in her mouth and sipped.

The flavour grabbed her right away. *I must have been
thirstier than I thought.* She grunted appreciatively and
sucked hard on the straws.

"I'm glad you like it," said Salvadore. "Soda-making is
a lost art. I figure somebody has to keep it up. So, where-
abouts are you and your not-boyfriend from?"

Her straws gurgled as she finished the ice cream soda.
She set the glass down and glared at his grin. "I have to go
to the bathroom." She turned her back on him.

The washroom was all shining tile. It smelled strongly
of cleaning fluid. You'd think somebody was desperate to

hide all evidence of what had happened here. She sniffed the air suspiciously before stepping into the stall.

A few minutes later, as Aurora grabbed some paper towels beside the sink to dry her hands, her eyes tracked up to a corkboard display of flyers advertising local dances and on-the-side home businesses. There was even a missing child poster, with a family photograph from happier times imploring the onlooker for information—

Aurora peered closer at the photograph. The wad of towels dropped to the floor. "Mom?!"

It was her mother, standing on the diving pier stretching out into Lake Winnipeg, wearing a swimsuit and holding a beach ball, grinning. Aurora remembered that grin. She remembered taking the photograph. What was it doing here?

Aurora's hand went to her mouth. "Mom!" She choked against the sudden rise of tears. When she looked at the photograph again, the picture showed a young girl beaming at the camera, holding a doll. She looked a bit like Britney.

Aurora rubbed her eyes and looked again, but the picture didn't change.

"This is just nuts," she muttered, turning to the mirror.

Her mother stood where her reflection should be.

Aurora stifled a shriek. Keeping her eyes on the mirror, she reached out behind her, but her hand met open air. She chanced a quick look over her shoulder, but she was alone in the washroom. She looked back at the mirror, and her mother was still there, gripping the edge of the sink, staring at her, mouth agape.

Then Aurora realized she couldn't see her own reflection in the mirror. The washroom her mother stood in had different tiles, and there was a shower.

Her mother was speaking to her. Shouting at her, but making no sound. Aurora could only read her mother's lips.

Aurora?

"Mom?"

What are you doing there? How did you—?

She was talking faster now. Aurora couldn't keep up.

"Mom, I can't hear you!" Aurora put her hands to her ears, then held them out, palms up.

Her mom kept shouting, but she shortened her sentences—Aurora could tell by the way her mouth put a weight on every word. Aurora peered into the mirror.

Look. Out. Danger.

Aurora leaned back from the mirror. She turned to look at the washroom door. When she turned back, her mother was gone.

She bit her lip, and touched the mirror, briefly. Then she turned and left the washroom, stepping carefully back into the store.

She heard the sizzle of breakfast and Salvadore scraping the grill. She focused on the front door and strode quickly but quietly down an aisle of shelves filled with canned vegetables.

Salvadore suddenly stood in her way. "Where are you going?"

She backed up and started down a different grocery aisle, only to have Salvadore block her path again. Her mouth went dry. *How is he doing that?*

"I'm just going to see how Polk's doing," she said. Then she thought: *That's a good question. Where is Polk?* She looked out the screen door. The car was there, attached to the gas pump with a nozzle, but Polk was nowhere to be seen. "Polk?" she shouted.

"I'm sure he'll be in presently," said Salvadore. "Have a seat—breakfast is almost ready."

"I want to stretch my legs."

Aurora tried to sidle to the left, only to have Salvadore mimic her. Her heart thumped. She had been stupid. Lulled into a false sense of security. Something had been telling her that something was wrong, but she hadn't realized what...

Then she realized. The sausages and eggs were sizzling on the grill, but she couldn't smell them. She could only smell cleaning fluid, and under that a hint of mildew.

Salvadore caught her frown and sniffed the air. "Hmm..."

Something rustled in his hair. Something crawled up the back of his shirt. Two spiders emerged, big as the palm of her hand. They stood on Salvadore's head and shoulder, looking at her.

A slow smile spread across his face. "Oops."

Aurora scrambled backwards and looked around wildly for a way to escape. He was between her and the door, but if she could run to one of the other aisles...

But as she turned, the world tilted beneath her feet. She grabbed one of the shelves, sending cans clattering across the floor. Her stomach lurched, and spots glittered before her eyes. She tried to haul herself upright, but nausea pushed down on her like an open hand. She turned towards the back but tripped over her own feet and fell. Salvadore caught her under the armpits.

"Most kidnappers don't think to do this." He nodded at the soda glass on the counter. "*Always* drug your target early. That way they don't have time to become suspicious."

Aurora opened her mouth to say something furious, but all that came out was a gurgle. She shoved herself away, staggered and fell into a display case. Cans rolled everywhere.

Salvadore kicked the cans aside. Gripping her shoulders, he pulled her into a sitting position and checked her over. She couldn't even hold up her head.

His goatee and smile filled her vision. "You'll live. Just take a rest; that's a good girl. Someone very important wants to talk to you."

Her vision went black.

CHAPTER FOUR:
IN A NAMELESS TOWN

AURORA WALKED HOME FROM SCHOOL ALONE, hands in the pockets of her new denim jacket, eyes on the ground. She followed the sidewalk without looking at the traffic lights.

She jumped when an arm reached out, barring her way.

"Whoa, there," said a bespectacled crossing guard. "Where's your mind at today?"

"Sorry," Aurora mumbled.

"Not as sorry as you would be if you just walked out into traffic," said the guard.

She looked up at him. His gaze met hers...

A small boy stands in the middle of the road, staring in terror at an oncoming dump truck.

"Never fear! I shall save you!" The crossing guard flies down from the rooftops, lands in front of the little boy, and raises his stop sign.

The truck driver applies the brakes. The horn blares. There is a squeal and the smell of burning rubber. The truck stops within inches of the two of them.

The little boy hugs the crossing guard's leg. "You saved me!"

The crossing guard beams. "Not to worry, son. All in a day's work for—"

Aurora smiled despite herself. The guard faced the road and held up his stop sign. Traffic stopped, and he grandly ushered her forward like royalty. Aurora curtsied and crossed the street. As she passed the guard, she said, "Thanks...Crossing Guard Man."

He stared at her, eyes wide. She walked on without looking back.

All the way home, Aurora thought about her strange new power. As she closed the front door and pulled off her coat, she wondered how, or if, she could tell her mom about it. Her mother hadn't included it in their "facts of life" discussion (which Aurora remembered in all of its excruciating, red-faced detail). She'd been smart enough not to tell any of the other kids that she could see their dreams. They just thought she was weird. If she told somebody, even her mom, they might think she was crazy. They might even lock her up.

But maybe I am crazy. Maybe I need to be locked up.

She heard her mom rummaging in the kitchen and shouted, "Mom! I'm home!"

"In here, honey!" her mom shouted back.

At her mother's voice, Aurora relaxed. *This is Mom I'm talking about. She'll know. She'll hug me and tell me that it's going to be all right, and it will.*

Aurora bounded into the kitchen and saw her mother putting groceries away. Mom hadn't even had time to change out of her work clothes. Takeout bags from Branigan's filled the room with their French-fry smell. Mom looked up as Aurora came in and beamed at her. "How was your day?"

"Okay, I guess. Another math quiz. I did all right."

"That's nice, honey!" Her mother put another grocery bag on the counter and pulled out a lime green and teal package. "Oh, and look what I got you from the store today." She presented it with a flourish. "Maxi pads!"

Aurora went pink. "Mom!"

Her mother clasped the package as though it was something precious. "Can't I be happy about my little girl growing up?"

"Sure, Mom, but—" Aurora shuddered. She snatched the package and tucked it under her arm. "Just don't let ·the neighbours hear, okay?"

Her mother grinned and turned back to the groceries. Aurora placed the package on the counter, then turned back to her mom, her hands clasped in front of her, knuckles whitening. "Mom?"

Head within the fridge, her mother said, "What is it, honey?"

Aurora brought her hands to her lips and steepled her fingers, but the words wouldn't come out. She opened her mouth, held it a moment, then shut it before opening it again. "Mom?"

"Yes?" The mayonnaise jar clunked against the shelf.

"Mom..." She took a deep breath. "Something strange... happened at school."

Her mother bumped her head on the top of the refrigerator compartment. She pulled herself up and looked at her daughter. "What happened, honey?"

"I...I was...talking to my friend, Anne. And I looked at her, and...I could see what she was thinking. She was jealous about my jacket," Aurora began. "And Miss Daultry... she dreams about teaching a class without any students in it. And the other kids—"

She looked up at her mother and into her mother's eyes.

...Dawn leaves a squat medical building, passing the sign bearing her name and title: Dr. Dawn Perrault, Psychologist/ Sleep Specialist. She crosses the asphalt patch towards the streetcar stop—

"Dawn," says a voice. "Don't go, Dawn."

A truck driver stands on the pavement in front of his black big rig, his arms folded. He wears black jeans, black cowboy boots, and a black shirt with a collar. His smile shines like the sun breaking from behind clouds.

"How do you know my name? Who are you?"

His chuckle resonates in her chest, and her breathing catches...

"Don't be afraid," he says.

"I'm not afraid!" She knows she should be. A strange man who knows her name, asking her aboard his truck. He's bigger than her. And yet—

"You don't have to if you don't want to," he says.

She wants to...

"Show me."

The truck drives into the night, faster and faster, breaking speed limits, but no one notices. The streetlights play off its shiny black exterior, fluttering off the mirrors, teasing the shadows like feathers. The wheels lift off. Wings catch the air.

The giant crow rises skyward, Dawn clasps the back of his neck...

Dawn nestles in an embrace of shadow.

Oh, God! Oh, God! Yes!

Aurora jerked back, looking at anything but her mother's eyes. *I shouldn't be able to look into people's private dreams like this! It's just* wrong!

Her mother stood by the refrigerator, her hand over her mouth. For a long moment, they stood on opposite sides of the kitchen, not looking at each other, not speaking.

Then her mother stepped forward. "Aurora, are you okay? What's wrong?" She opened her arms. "Come here, honey."

Aurora ran into her mother's arms.

"What's *really* happening, honey?" said her mom in her ear.

"It was weird…" Aurora's voice was muffled in her mother's sweater. "It was a weird...dream! Yeah. A weird dream." She gulped. "Weirdest dream ever."

"A dream." Her mother held Aurora out to look at her face. Her mom's face was ashen, but she nodded. "Th-that's...horrible, honey. But it was *just* a dream. You know that, right? You don't have to dream that again if you don't want to."

"No," said Aurora, hugging her mom close again. "No. I don't want to."

They ate dinner in silence.

The next day, Aurora saw her mother hang the first spirit ball on their front door.

Aurora struggled awake from only the second bout of sleep she could remember since she was twelve.

Like the first, this one left her feeling anything but refreshed. Her head ached, and her mouth tasted bitter and sticky. She groaned, kept her eyes closed, and tried to touch her forehead. When her hand remained firmly planted behind her back, she opened her eyes.

Who'd turned out the lights?

She blinked until her eyes adjusted to the darkness. She gagged at the smell. No cleaning fluid here, just rotting wood, ancient mothballs, and stale urine.

What little light there was trickled through a cracked window that was caked with dirt. She was lying on her side in a bathroom—no, the *same* bathroom, the one she'd seen Mom in. The notice board hung askew on the wall, notices faded or ripped away, but with the photo of the missing girl still smiling at her. The sink and toilet were where she'd first seen them. The toilet looked...

"Ugh!"

And she'd used it.

The mirror was spotted and cracked. Tiles were missing on the floor and walls. The bathroom seemed to have aged twenty years in an instant. *Or maybe this was just what it had always looked like, covered up by an illusion of cleanliness, just like the smell of cleaning fluid that had been all over this place.*

The oddness of it all stopped her for a moment. Then, when she tried to pick herself up off the floor, she remembered that she couldn't move her hands from behind her. She looked down at herself and gasped.

Shiny grey bands wrapped around her knees and ankles,

biting into her jeans. The pressure on her wrists behind her told her that they were bound as well.

Her heart pounded and her breathing quickened. *He's tied me up! Tied me up like some damsel in distress!*

But he hadn't gagged her. Which meant he didn't expect anyone around to hear her yell. He was probably right, which sucked. But though nobody else could hear her yell, *he* could. And if he realized that she was awake, he could stop her from escaping before she'd even started.

So, Aurora held her breath, then let it out slowly. As her racing heart eased, she thought, *Right. The first thing I have to do is keep quiet. And the next thing I have to do is get myself free. Quickly and quietly.*

Aurora rolled onto her back and sat up. She leaned against a wall that sagged under her weight as she took stock of things. She looked for knots on her ropes and found none.

They weren't ropes at all, but shiny, silky strands, thinner than hair, but so many, they held her with the strength of steel. They were like...

Spider silk.

Aurora looked up and caught movement in the gloom. Salvadore's two spiders crouched on the bathroom tiles by the toilet stall. You couldn't tell where spiders were looking so surely they weren't looking at her, right?

They were looking at her.

A quick glance around the bathroom told her that, other than the spiders, she was alone. She looked at the spiders again. They looked back.

No, she thought. *You can drug me, tie me up and stick me in a dirty bathroom somewhere, but being guarded by spiders is where I draw the line.*

With a grunt, she pushed herself up the wall to her feet. Bound ankle and knee, with her wrists tied behind her, she hopped menacingly towards the watching spiders. They quivered, then scuttled away.

"Oh, no, you don't!" Aurora judged the last leap on the fly. Something squelched beneath her shoes. "Yes!" Her cry of joy turned to an "Eep!" as momentum tipped her forward. The dividing wall between the toilet and sink loomed in her vision. With her hands tied behind her back, there was nothing she could do.

The soggy drywall crunched under her forehead. She sank to her knees, face sliding down the mouldy surface, and lay propped there for a while.

"Ow..."

She pushed herself away and looked the false wall up and down. The tiles were cracked near the base and showed exposed edges. That would be perfect for cutting her bonds. Unfortunately, the wall was also surrounded by a yellowish puddle of suspicious-smelling water, but a damsel had to do what a damsel had to do. She turned around, leaned against the wall and slid down, settling into the puddle. She grimaced as the smelly water—she hoped it was water—soaked her jeans, and began rubbing her bound wrists with the ragged edge of a broken tile. Minutes later, the bonds came apart.

She grunted triumphantly and brought her hands around to rub the pins and needles out of them. Then she set about tearing at the strands binding her knees and ankles, using fingers and sometimes teeth. She spat out mashed spider silk and was back on her feet, dripping but smiling smugly. *Aurora Perrault, damsel in distress? No friggin' way!*

Then she frowned. *Where's Polk? How long have I been out? He should have noticed something wrong by now.*

Her frown deepened. *He would. And while he might be lazy, he'd try to do something about it.*

So, where is he?

Her job had just become a lot harder.

She tiptoed to the bathroom door, gripped the door handle and listened for voices.

Salvadore was speaking in the next room, but he seemed to be alone. At least, she couldn't hear a second voice.

She crept out of the bathroom, careful to close the door behind her without the doorknob clicking. Crouching low, she eased forward.

"Yes, she's here," Salvadore said. "I got her all packed up and waiting for you."

Aurora paused at the end of the housewares aisle and peered down it towards the front of the store. Salvadore was standing at the cash register, leaning on the counter with his back to her, his hand cupped to his ear.

He drew up sharply. "I didn't hurt her." There was a squabble on the other end of the line. "I didn't. Yes, she is restrained." More squabbles. "Look, she wasn't going to come quietly!"

Aurora ran her gaze across the open space between her and Salvadore. There were three aisles of groceries on her right, but the rest of the space was open except for an abandoned display bin that had once held candy bars. Above Salvadore, a security mirror displayed the whole store. Aurora could see herself creeping up in its age-scarred surface, but Salvadore was too engrossed in his call to look up.

There was a burst of babble on the other end of the line.

"Look," snapped Salvadore, "she doesn't know the truth. She just thinks she's a normal kid—there's no way she'd believe the truth, especially if *I* was the one to tell her. So, I thought I'd leave the explanation to you."

The squabbling intensified again. Salvadore raised his other hand in a futile gesture to ward it off.

Aurora crept past one shelf and into the cover of another aisle. She peered out into the open area and stepped out again. The front door was closer but still too far away for her to chance a run.

"Will you listen to me?" Salvadore said, finally cutting in. "I gave you my word of honour that I would find her and that she would not be the worse for wear. You know how much my word is worth."

There was a brief squabble. Salvadore straightened up angrily. "Very funny! Look, you come and untie her, you talk to her, and soon you'll have her wrapped around your little finger. I assure you. Okay?"

There was a grumpy mumble at the other end, but Sal-vadore nodded. "Good." He half-turned towards the store. Aurora froze, but he turned back. "Wait, what? The other one? I had to get him out of the way. In the course of duty, you understand?"

A brief squabble.

"Why?" echoed Salvadore. "Well, for one thing, he's bigger than her and a lot harder to dupe, that's why! I had to take stronger measures." A short gabble. "Good! Good to know."

There was a click. Salvadore dropped his empty hand to his side. He cracked his knuckles. "I'd better go check up on Charlotte, Arabella, and my charming little prisoner." Smiling, he turned around.

And Aurora brained him with the cast-iron frying pan she'd picked up in aisle three.

Aurora burst out of the general store and blinked at the sudden brightness. The car was where they'd left it, by the gas pumps, which now looked even older and more sunbleached, their logos faded to nothing. The nozzle stuck in their car was brown with rust. Aurora stepped around the car and tried the pump. It wasn't working. The nozzle left brown stains on her palms.

She looked around. The general store sagged where minutes—or maybe hours—ago it had stood tall. The boards on the windows were coming off their nails and swinging in the wind. The barn at the top of the hill was more frame than walls. It had all been a great big fake.

But how? I saw it. I smelled it.

She clenched her fists. *Another dream out to get me. When did I slip into it? If these dreams can catch me that easily, how can I even begin to defend myself?*

"Polk?" Her words echoed back at her. "Polk!"

She looked around, then down at her stained hands. She hooked the nozzle back on the gas pump, only for the hose to break off and flop to the ground. She walked around the store. "Polk!"

The fields around the store grew wild: barley mixed with saskatoons and wild grasses. Aurora's feet crunched on the gravel. She passed a pile of rusted car parts. The wind brushed back her hair. The only sound was the rustle and snap of the dirty plastic bags rising and falling above the saskatoons, caught in their never-ending updraft.

"Polk!" she shouted again.

She reached the back of the store and found him sprawled on the ground. She ran to him. "Polk!"

He was out cold, eyes closed, eyelids fluttering. She put her ear close to his mouth. He was breathing, but barely.

Aurora checked him over for injury, but there were no broken bones. No marks whatsoever, except a slight purple-red, like the start of a bruise, over his mouth and nose. Then what had knocked him out? The ground was scuffled around him, but there was only one set of footprints: his.

She leaned close and shook him by the shoulders. "Polk? Polk! Wake up!"

He mumbled and tried to roll over in his sleep.

She shook him harder. "Polk!"

He came to, yelling, clawing at unseen monsters near his face. She caught his wrists. "Polk! Polk! It's just me!"

He stopped struggling and blinked at her. "Aurora?" He looked past her, and his eyes widened. "Look out!"

"What—?" She looked over her shoulder.

Smack! She recoiled as one of the plastic bags swept out

of the air and caught her across the cheek and shoulder. She beat at it, but it clung to her.

Smack! Slap! Two more plastic bags hit her: one across the chest and one across her chin.

Slap! This one swept over her face. She felt it wrap around her head and tighten as if it was knotted behind her. She gasped and sucked in plastic.

Panic hit her, and she flailed, but she couldn't see, she couldn't grapple with anything, and she couldn't breathe. She desperately tried to suck in air, but the plastic made a taut drum over her gaping mouth. Her vision darkened.

Fingers clawed at her head, scratched her ear, and pulled the bag free. The plastic stuck like flypaper. Polk tried to throw it away, but it wrapped itself around his fingers and knotted over the back of his hand.

"Polk—" she started, then yelled as another bag slapped and tightened across *his* face until he looked like a plastic mannequin. He staggered and flailed at the plastic stretched across his mouth, his fingers useless under their plastic binding. Aurora grabbed an edge and yanked, her fingernails drawing blood across Polk's cheeks. She clutched the fluttering thing and shoved it under her foot. She saw a small fieldstone within reach and slammed it on top. The bag struggled to rise, but the rock held firm.

She looked back in time to see more bags swooping down, but Polk was ready. He batted them away. She tore off the bag that was beating at her chest and stuffed it under another fieldstone. They stood back to back, hands raised warily as the plastic bags circled. They swatted and clawed at any that swooped close.

Aurora shouted at the bags and the wind. "Leave us alone!"

The bags ducked and weaved for an opening, but Polk and Aurora stood ready to fend off any attack. Then the wind abruptly calmed, leaving the bags hovering in midair a moment, before another gust swept them away, and they vanished into the fields of barley.

Aurora and Polk stayed where they were, backs touching, arms raised. After a long moment, Aurora realized her hands were shaking. She lowered her arms. They looked at each other.

"Are you okay?" Aurora asked.

Polk bent over gasping, pressing his hands to his knees. He nodded. "More or less."

She looked across the fields, to see if any other danger was lying in wait. If there was, she couldn't see it. "Let's get out of here." She started toward the front of the store.

Polk followed her, staying close. "Where's that guy?" he asked as the gravel crunched. "Salvadore?"

"Unconscious. At least, I hope so. I bashed him on the head with a frying pan."

Polk whooped. "Way to go!"

The front of the store was as she'd left it. There was no sound but the wind, a low ghostly moan. They stopped at the station wagon.

"I couldn't get the pumps to work," said Polk.

"That's because there's no gas."

He looked up and down the road and raised his hands. "This is the only place around for miles, and we're nearly empty. What do we do?"

Aurora opened the car door. "Just get in and go."

Polk hesitated. "But we haven't brought anything. We've no supplies."

"Polk," she said irritably, "there's nothing here. It's just a trap. We've got to go."

"No." He pushed away from the car. "We're almost out of gas. If we run out in the middle of nowhere, we should at least have water."

"Salvadore's in there!"

"It's two against one, now, and we know what to expect." He turned towards the front door.

A change in the silence made Aurora hesitate before she followed him. She listened. A gentle roar started up at the edge of hearing and rose steadily. It could be an engine. In a moment, she'd know for sure, but by then it might be too late.

She looked up the road the way they had come. A small cloud of yellow-grey dust was rising on the horizon, almost lost among the heat shimmers coming off the asphalt.

"Polk!" she shouted. She pointed up the road. "We've got to go, now!"

He looked at the northern horizon, then came down the front steps. "Hey, this is lucky. We could use them as back-up and then hitch a ride out of here."

She shook her head. *This is wrong. It's more than just drugged ice cream sodas and demonic plastic bags. This isn't a matter of three strikes, and you're out. That truck, whatever it is, is the only vehicle we've seen on this road since running from Cooper's Corners. That can't be a coincidence. But how can I convince Polk when he's just so oblivious?*

A thought struck her, and she leaned against the car. "Polk, four points. What is it?"

He closed his eyes automatically. "It's a rig." He tilted his head. "It will be black, with…" He frowned. "That's strange… I can't tell—"

Just like that rig that brought the dark man and his vision of crows. Aurora opened her door wider and slid in. "Polk, get in, we're leaving!" She fumbled with the ignition, and the car grumbled to life. "Get in, dammit!"

Polk ducked into the passenger seat and slammed his door. "What are you doing? We'll end up stuck on the side of the road, sitting ducks!"

"We'll have to hide the car." Aurora put the car in gear.

"Hide?" Polk waved a hand at the wide-open landscape. Nothing was more than chest height. "Where?"

The car hit the road with a spray of gravel. The low-gas indicator on the dashboard began to flash and ding. "I know, I know," Aurora muttered.

They topped a ridge and stared down at a small valley barely fifty metres wide. A short bridge over a narrow creek lay at the bottom.

"There!" Aurora pointed.

"Where?"

Aurora twisted the wheel, and the station wagon careened off the road. Polk clutched the handle above the door. The car jounced. Branches beat against the front grille. Aurora twisted the wheel, and the car staggered onto the creek bed, which was not much more than a strip of mud. She kept twisting, and the roadway came back into view. The creek passed through a culvert barely as tall and wide as the car. Aurora revved the engine. The wheels spun, producing a wake in the muddy water like a motorboat.

Polk sat up in his seat and grabbed for more handholds. "Oh, no."

"Oh, yes," said Aurora, her face grim.

Polk yelled as the car smashed into the culvert. The side mirrors sheared off. The sides of the car squealed like fingernails on a chalkboard. Sparks flew from the corrugated metal of the culvert. Aurora and Polk pitched forward. The airbags billowed out to catch them.

There was a moment of near-silence as Aurora and Polk sat, gasping. Then Aurora shoved the airbag away and turned off the ignition.

"There," she breathed. "We're hidden."

Polk tried the car door. It wouldn't open. "We're also stuck."

She nodded over her shoulder. "Hello? We're in a station wagon!"

He turned around. Behind the back seats was the station wagon's hatch. It was shaded by the top of the culvert.

"Let's go," she said.

They crawled up the bank and along the drainage ditch, keeping low. They stopped when the abandoned store came into view. The yellow-brown cloud had materialized into a black ten-wheeler rig, roaring up the road towards them. Its trailer stretched back, also black, but strangely fuzzy in the heat shimmers. Aurora remembered it from the day before all this started. *So, it hadn't been just a dream.*

"Why are we running from a truck?" Polk muttered.

"That truck was in my dream."

"So, we're dreaming, now?" he asked.

That's a good question, thought Aurora. *But I woke up from the dream that made me think the general store wasn't an abandoned relic. Have I slipped back in? When? It's getting hard to tell what's real and what isn't.*

"Let's just keep out of sight, okay?" she muttered.

The truck pulled up in front of the general store and cut its engines. The door opened, and a black figure eased out, taking the steps slowly, before jumping to the ground. The man straightened up. Aurora recognized him from the diner—and from her mother's dream three years ago. Black hair, black shirt, black pants, black boots. He sucked in the light around him. She could feel the pull from where she crouched.

The black figure turned sharply and scanned the distance all around. Aurora and Polk pulled their heads down and held their breath.

Then, with a crunch of gravel, the black figure strode into the general store. The screen door slammed shut behind him. Silence fell.

Aurora peered out from their hiding place. Polk pinched her arm. She gasped and slapped him in the back of the head. "Ow!"

He winced. "Ow! I was just trying to wake you."

"When I want your help, I'll ask for it! Now be quiet!"

A howl burst from the general store and rose until it made Aurora want to cover her ears. It cut off suddenly as the screen door opened and Salvadore came half-flying, half-stumbling out. He staggered down the stairs, clutching his forehead from where Aurora had brained him, and ran face-first into the side of the black rig.

Salvadore turned as the screen door opened again. He stood by the rig, crouched, hands clasped, talking a mile a minute and keeping his head low. The black-clad figure grabbed him by the collar and manhandled him into the passenger side of the cab.

Then, striding around to the driver's side of the rig, the man in black climbed into the truck and slammed the door. The engine roared to life, and the black rig eased onto the road and picked up speed. Aurora and Polk pulled deeper into their hiding place as the rig topped the ridge, but it didn't stop. It passed, its edges blurred and fluttering. Peering up, Aurora realized that the whole trailer was nothing more than a flock of crows, keeping pace with the rig, and keeping the shape of the truck. Half a dozen plastic bags sailed past in its wake.

They crouched in hiding until the roar faded into the distance. The dust settled around them like hot, dry snow. When the only sound was the wind rustling the grasses around them, Aurora stood up and walked out. She stood in the centre of the roadway, staring at where the truck had gone.

Polk followed her, standing on the shoulder of the road, looking back and forth along its length. "Was that truck made of—?"

"Yes."

"Are we dreaming?"

Aurora pinched her arm, winced, then pinched her arm again. Nothing happened. "I don't know." Engines sighed overhead and she looked up. High above them, a distant plane left a thin contrail across the cornflower-blue sky, like a visitor from the land of normal. She looked down again. "I don't think so."

"Huh." Polk looked both ways along the roadway again. "Your dreams are chasing us."

"I know."

"They're between us and where we want to go."

"Yes."

He stuffed his hands in his denim jacket pockets. "So, what do we do?"

Aurora took several long, deep breaths. "We have to find another way to Saskatoon."

She looked out across the countryside. In the heat of the rising sun, the air started to shimmer.

CHAPTER FIVE:
AS THE CROW FLIES

AURORA SLAMMED INTO DREAMS EVERY TIME she looked a classmate in the eye. By the end of the first week, she was sick with it. At recess, she sat in a window well at the base of the school, rolling a tennis ball between her feet. Laughter echoed around her. Roger and his muscle crew stumbled into view, cackling as they wrestled, staggering close to Aurora. She looked away.

Roger righted himself and shoved his friends away. They darted off, laughing. Roger leered at Aurora. She kept her gaze on the ground. When he ran off, Aurora glared at his back. Then she went back to kicking the tennis ball between her feet.

"Hey!" The sound of Albijana's aggrieved voice made Aurora look up.

At the school gate, Albijana stood trembling with frustration as Roger turned her red rubber ball over in his hands.

"Cool ball," he said, twisting out of her reach. "I bet if you bounce it really hard, it could go really high."

"Give it back!" Albijana wailed.

"Just let me test it." Roger pretended to bounce the ball

on the ground, then hauled back and tossed the ball with all his might. It sailed high into the air, clearing the third-storey windows of the school before disappearing above the roofline.

Roger grinned at Albijana. "Yup. It goes really high."

His friends laughed. Albijana stood rigid, fists clenched. Then she said something in Arabic. One of her friends heard it and gasped.

Roger sneered at her. "Out of my way, you little monkey."

People stopped and stared, but Roger pushed past Albijana and walked away. The girl turned and walked to the school wall, her shoulders slumped and her head down. She walked right up to Aurora without looking and would have bumped into her if Aurora hadn't cleared her throat.

Albijana jumped back. "I'm sorry!"

Aurora gave her a small smile. "It's okay." She shifted over to one side of the window well, making room. Albijana hesitated then sat down on the concrete sill.

"Talk to a caretaker," said Aurora. "He can go to the roof and get it."

Albijana sniffed. "Okay."

They waited in silence for the school bell to ring.

Aurora looked at Albijana's light brown skin and long, dark hair. "Did they bomb your country?"

Albijana looked at her sharply.

Aurora swallowed. "I just...I read—"

"Yes," said Albijana, her eyes dark. Aurora shook the sound of air raid sirens out of her head.

"Why?" Albijana asked.

"I just…I mean, I wanted to know. You seemed…it's—"

Albijana turned away. "Yes," she said again. "I hate it. I hate them."

"But you're safe here," said Aurora quietly.

Albijana shook her head. She picked up a pebble and turned it around in her fingers. "They're in my dreams. The bombs. The soldiers. Everybody running away. They won't stop."

Silence stretched.

"You know," said Aurora carefully. "It's…just a dream."

"It's not a dream!" Albijana threw the stone to the ground. "It's not! It happened! It…" Her voice trailed off and she bit her lip.

"I know it happened," said Aurora quickly. "But when you go back in your dreams, it's still a dream. It's not real in your dreams."

"It *feels* real." Albijana tossed the pebble aside. "They say…if you die in your dreams, you die in real life."

"But…you don't have to do what the dreams tell you to do."

Albijana frowned at her, but she didn't turn away.

"Look," said Aurora, "My mother knows dreams. She says they're all the same: they take place in your head. It's all a part of your imagination. We use our imagination all the time, right? We play rocket ships on the monkey bars. We play fortress on the playground equipment. If we can make things into other things in our imagination, why not in our dreams?"

Albijana's brow furrowed.

"Try it," said Aurora. "Tell your dreams that you won't

dream this anymore. Tell your dreams that you're taking over and doing what *you* want."

The school bell rang. Albijana stood up, still frowning. She walked to the doors without looking back.

❧

Aurora and Polk decided to explore the abandoned store first.

The screen door came off its hinges when Polk pulled on it. Inside, they covered their mouths and noses at the overpowering smell of mildew. Sunlight fell in shafts from gaps in the boards hammered over the windows. The floor was white, except for the dark footprints Aurora and Salvadore had left behind in the dust.

Aurora picked up a package of licorice off its display rack, sniffed it, then smacked it against the cash counter. It shattered into a million pieces.

"There's nothing here." She tossed the rest of the package aside.

"There's got to be something." Polk blew a cloud of dust off a can of beans and turned it in his hands before holding it out to her. "See? This doesn't expire for another month."

"Oh, goody."

Aurora wandered around the store, raising clouds of dust. The cash register was open, its display showing a tab marked "No Sale." The drawer was empty. Then her foot hit something beneath the cash register. It was a cardboard pallet half-full of water bottles.

She knelt down. "Polk! Over here!"

Polk rushed over and did a little shuffle of triumph. "That's exactly what I was hoping for." He picked up a bottle, peered at it, and shook it. "Looks okay." He tossed her one.

She caught it, unscrewed the cap and took a swig, which became a chug. She gulped down the water and tossed the empty bottle aside, wiping her mouth with the back of her hand. "It's good," she said.

"Worth looking around after all?"

"Yeah, yeah."

Polk's grin faded. "How on earth are we going to carry all this?"

They found a dusty canvas bag tucked in the drawer under the broken cash register. They packed all the water they could into it. This filled the bag halfway and they were still able to carry it. Then they argued over the beans.

"They're useless, heavy, and frankly disgusting," said Aurora, her hands on her hips, wrinkling her nose as Polk waved a can in front of her.

"We're going to have to eat, too, you know."

"I'll wait."

"You'll starve."

"I'm not going to starve!"

Polk heaved a long-suffering sigh.

She snatched the canvas bag. "Okay, you want beans? Have some beans!" She shoved an entire shelf full of cans into the canvas bag and handed it to him. Polk took the bag and dropped it on his foot.

Aurora stood with arms folded as Polk hopped about.

He rubbed his toe. "Thanks a million!" He dug into the

bag and plunked half the cans back on the shelf. He hefted the bag in front of her. "Compromise?"

She weighed it in her hand. "You promise to carry this whenever I get tired?"

"Sure."

"Deal."

They picked up a can opener and plastic spoons from the housewares aisle and headed for the front door. At the front stood a rack of baseball caps. Polk picked one up and blew off a cloud of dust that made Aurora choke. He picked up another, beat the dust off against his pant leg, and handed it to her.

Aurora sneered at it. It was a denim cap with the Playboy logo on it. "I'm not wearing that!"

"In this weather, it's that or sunstroke."

Aurora grabbed the cap and tossed it away. She flipped through the rack and found a white cap with a Baltimore Ravens football logo on it. She beat the dust off and pulled it on.

Polk pulled on his hat. It was black and had the initials N.Y.P.D. stitched across it. "Ready?"

Aurora looked out the door at the wide, rolling landscape, and was struck again with the sense of being one of the last two humans in existence. The air in the store was heating up as fast as an oven. Outside, waves of heat quivered above the ground.

Out in that with only beans and water? What are we doing?

And what the hell am I doing getting Polk involved?

Polk turned to step outside, but she grabbed the doorframe, blocking him. He frowned at her. "What?"

"Where do you think you're going?"

He looked from her to the road and back again. "Saskatoon, like you said." He drew back from her, and his frown deepened. "With you."

Aurora stepped into the sunlight and gripped both sides of the door frame. "You don't have to." She pushed out her words. "If Matron's right, and it's me they're after, then you could just walk away, and be safe. So, why don't you be safe? As long as you're next to me, they're after you as well."

He shook his head. "No way. You're going to hike in a Saskatchewan heat wave? Miles from anywhere? That's insane! You might as well walk the Sahara."

"It's not that bad!"

"Is too!"

"Polk, don't go all Prince Charming on me. You don't have the looks, and you don't have the sword. This is between me and whoever is following me."

He reddened. "Prince Charming? Is that why you think I'm doing this? You want me to walk away while you face it all alone? You're insane! How can you think I'd do that, to anyone?"

"You could go see if Matron's all right," she said quietly.

They both winced. It was cruel to say that, but it needed saying. With the dark man focused on her, Matron could be okay for all they knew. But they didn't know. And Polk would want to know at least as much as she did.

He stood a long minute, his eyes closed. Then he looked up and looked her in the eye.

Polk walks through the wheat, his heart beating faster.

Aurora blinked the dream away and focused on Polk's forehead.

He took a deep breath. "I'm. Coming. With. You." He gave a final nod.

Aurora couldn't help smiling. "Okay. Thanks." She let go of the door frame. "Let's go."

"I'd bake in Prince Charming's armour, anyway," he muttered. He pulled the cloth straps of the canvas sack over each shoulder and wore the bag like a backpack.

They climbed down the steps, walked back to the crest of the hill and looked down the road. The wind was still. The sun beat down from halfway up the eastern horizon. The sky had opened into a crystal-clear cornflower blue.

Polk shaded his eyes. They strained to peer at the road's vanishing point. Then Aurora saw it: a black speck in the sky, circling above the road. She strained her ears and heard the faint cry of crows.

"They're guarding the road."

"That could be anything," said Polk. But he took a step back.

"They're guarding the road. It's what I'd do."

"So...what?"

Aurora watched the distant crows. "Let's follow the creek."

⚶

They followed the muddy bank. The sun rose higher, and the shadows disappeared. Their pace slowed. Aurora pulled off her cap and wiped the sweat from her forehead.

In the silence, her mind tumbled. *Why me?* she thought. *What do they want with me?*

"You okay?" Polk's voice derailed her train of thought.

"What?"

"You're not watching where you're going." He was holding her by the elbow, guiding her away from the stream.

She sighed. "Why are they chasing me, Polk?"

"Maybe you shouldn't think about that too hard. Maybe focus on walking through this heat instead?"

"But it makes no sense." Aurora looked back. "Maybe I should go back and ask them."

"Yeah. Maybe they can help you pick out a good fabric for your sacrificial robe."

"Maybe if it's something I could give them, they'd stop—"

Matron's words echoed in her head. *You can't let him take you, girl! It'll be disaster if he does!* Whatever it was they wanted, it was no small thing.

"But why me?" She grimaced at the whine she heard in her voice. "I mean, trying to grab me in my dreams? Attacking us with crows and plastic bags?"

Polk nodded. "It seems a lot just to grab some young waitress, especially when there are plenty of prettier ones out there—*ow!*"

He staggered back from her punch to his shoulder and planted his foot in the stream. He shook it out. "Thanks."

"You're welcome."

He walked on with a step, shake-water-off, step, shake-water-off, step. Aurora stifled a laugh.

104

Polk's right, though, she thought. *A fifteen—almost sixteen—year-old waitress in some remote corner of Saskatchewan? It was ludicrous. What's so special about me—?*

She stopped in her tracks. *Oh. The dream thing.*

Polk stopped and turned back. "Aurora?"

The dream thing. That has to be it. It's the only thing that marks me off as special. But how could they know? I haven't told anyone about my abilities, not outright. And the one person who'd experienced them—she flinched at the memory of Salvadore—*was hardly in any condition to tell anyone.*

But Mom knew.

"Get stuck in the mud?" Polk grinned. "Hey, are you okay?"

She drew her breath in. Her hands clenched into fists. "Damn it!" she yelled. Starlings burst out of the flowers and into the sky.

Polk whirled, looking for attackers rushing towards them. "I thought we were supposed to stay in hiding!"

Aurora stomped her feet. "She knew! My mom knew! She shoved me here; she played with my memory to keep me 'safe.' She knew I was special enough that somebody wanted me, and she damn well never told me!"

Polk let the canvas bag slip from his shoulders. "Aurora, calm down."

She balled her hands into fists. She clenched her jaw and tried to take a cleansing breath.

Then her mind caught up to her mouth. She looked up at Polk, horrified. She'd been reckless.

"Aurora? What's wrong?" His sardonic smile was gone.

This was Polk. Her best friend in Cooper's Corners.

The only person who'd made the place bearable. And he'd walked with her this far.

"I know why they're after me, Polk," she said. "I've never told anybody this before, but...I can see people's dreams."

There was a long moment of silence. Polk stared at her. Aurora tried again. "I mean, I can see what people are dreaming when I look them in the eye."

His eyes flickered aside, but he still said nothing.

"Have you gotten through your wheatfield yet?"

"Oh, crap!" He lunged away from her, covering his eyes. "Does privacy mean nothing to you?"

"I can't help it!" she yelled. "I can't control it. It just happens."

He lowered his hand and looked at her warily. "Oh." Then, more seriously, "Oh! That can not be fun."

She threw up her hands. "Tell me about it. For the past three years, I've wanted to punch Jake Ransom's face in. That's what I like about your dreams, Polk: I don't feel the need to take a shower after."

He straightened up but still kept his gaze just out of eye contact. "Okay. I'll take that as a compliment. I think. How long have you...been able to do this?"

"Since my first period."

He ducked his head. "Too much information!"

"You asked."

He shook his head, looking stunned. "So, you can see people's dreams. That's...neat, I guess." He caught her look. "Or, maybe not. How do you know that's why they're after you?"

"They're attacking me in dreams, and I can read dreams—that isn't enough of a connection?" She continued more quietly. "My mom knew something. She knew that people were after me, and she sent me here to live with Aunt Matron."

"I always thought you were an orphan."

"I might as well be. She played with my memories to keep me here. Tried to make me forget my life in Winnipeg." She clenched her fists. "Polk, this is important. Tell me how you know me. How long have you known me?"

Polk opened his mouth, then closed it. "About three and a half years. Aurora, this is too weird for me. Do we really have to talk about this out here—?"

"Three years?" Aurora echoed. "Not twelve or fifteen? I look at you and I say to myself, this is a boy I grew up with; from the moment we got up and toddled around. This is a boy I went to kindergarten with. But only the last three years have been real."

She realized, with a sudden jerk of her heart, that she felt robbed to be losing those memories of Polk.

"You came...to live with us...three and a half years ago," said Polk at last, thinking hard and choosing his words with care. "Matron told me you were an orphan and that we were taking you in. She told me not to talk about your mother...because it was too painful for you."

"Or because it could have brought the memories back." She looked up at him, marvelling that, for three years, this secret hadn't slipped out. Polk hadn't once said something like, "Hey, you remember when you came to Cooper's Corners, three years ago?"

"Maybe they played with your memories too," she said.

"You'd think I'd remember that."

She shook her head. His grin faded.

"That's got to be it," she said. "It's the only thing that makes me special. They want me because I can see into people's dreams."

"Why?"

"I don't know. Matron did everything she could to make sure I didn't find out. Maybe this person in Saskatoon can tell me." She set her teeth. "I can't believe my mom wouldn't tell me!"

"Okay," said Polk. "My next big question: what exactly can we do with this information when we're out here?"

Aurora looked around, at the meandering strip of mud that passed for a creek, at the sea of brush and flowers that stretched to the horizon, at the blue dome of the sky. Her shoulders sagged. "Nothing. Let's keep going." She pushed past Polk.

He shrugged on the canvas bag and fell into step beside her, but she hardly noticed him.

Mom knew about me. The words rolled around in her head. *She knew.*

*

The sun rose too high for the creek's shallow banks to provide any shade. They trudged on. Aurora noticed they were approaching a low ridge running along the northeastern horizon. As they rounded a bend in the stream, they saw that the ridge crossed the creek, with a bridge that looked like a platform on stilts.

Aurora squinted at it. "That's too small to be a road bridge."

"Maybe it's a cattle-crossing or something," said Polk.

There were no farmhouses in sight. The only structures were the bridge, the ridge (which didn't look natural), and a line of power poles stretching into the distance.

Polk staggered.

Aurora frowned at him. "You wait here. I'll take a look around."

Leaving Polk puffing beside the creek, Aurora clawed her way up the embankment and poked her head above the bridge, feeling like a prairie dog peering out from its den. Her vision was blocked by a low wall of iron. She craned her head higher and saw that the low wall was actually a rail. Two ribbons of rusted steel curved away in either direction, drawing together as they reached the vanishing point.

"Huh," she said, and ducked down.

"It's a rail line," she called to Polk. "And it's heading south."

Polk looked up from where he sat slumped on the bank. "So?"

She looked up and down the run of the creek. "The creek was heading east," she said, "and now it's heading north-east. Saskatoon's south, so we're moving away from where we want to go." Then she focused on Polk. "Are you okay?"

He looked up at her, breathing heavily. "Me? I'm fine! Fine. So, east or south?"

Sweat cut lines in the dust on his face. His white

T-shirt was grey and soggy. Aurora's frown deepened as she came down the embankment. "You want me to carry the bag?"

"What?" He straightened up sharply. "No, I can handle it. Come on! Let's keep moving."

"I'd like some water, please."

Polk sagged with relief and slipped the cloth straps off his shoulders. He rummaged through the sack and brought out two bottles. He handed her one and twisted the cap off the other.

"Hey." She caught him with the bottle halfway to his mouth. "Drink slowly. Don't choke yourself."

They both drank. Then they stood looking at the sack full of more water. It was tempting but they decided to save it for later. Polk hefted the straps over his shoulders.

"You want me to carry that?" asked Aurora. "It's been a couple of hours."

"I'm fine. I'm here to help, you know." He grinned at her. "I swore to protect you."

Aurora rolled her eyes.

"I did! Placed my hand on the Good Book and everything! Anybody who comes after you has to get through me first. I also carry your bags."

"C'mon, Polk. It's been hours. I should take a turn too."

"I said, I'm okay!" He slipped and fell forward. One of the cans rolled out of the bag and thwacked him in the back of his head. "Ow!"

Aurora scrambled over and caught the bag before more of its contents could spill onto Polk. He looked up at her, dazed. "Okay," he said. "You can carry it a bit."

They followed the tracks south. The rails were rusted, but the gravel was well groomed. Walking from tie to tie, they picked up the pace. Aurora puffed with the canvas sack on her back. How had Polk managed to carry this the entire morning? Sometimes it felt as though she could point her toes, and it would drive her into the ground like a nail.

She let her hands drop to her sides. Her left hand brushed against Polk's. Their hands jerked apart as though they'd felt a shock. On they plodded. The ribbons of iron shimmered, making Aurora think of water. Again, her hand brushed Polk's. This time they didn't pull away. After a moment, she took his hand. Polk gave it a squeeze. They brought their heads down and pushed forward.

The afternoon disappeared into a haze of heat.

As the sun set, and they ambled around a curve on the rail embankment, the land ahead dropped away. They looked out on rolling scrublands full of grass and flowers. Aurora groaned at the sight of mile after mile of unpaved ground. Damned nature!

But as she took a few more steps, and more of the landscape pulled into view, her breath caught.

At first, she thought it was another mirage. But as she walked, she could see this was no mirage. The sun glittered on a sparkling mirror, a slough of water that stretched out in a circle a hundred metres wide, reflecting so brightly that they had to shield their eyes.

Aurora stopped. Polk stopped too. They stood there, breathing hard, transfixed by the glittering water, but too tired to move or speak.

"Oh…that's *so* tempting," Aurora moaned at last.

"Yeah," said Polk.

She looked up at him. "Want a swim?"

He thought about it. "Aren't we supposed to be on the run?"

They looked at the slough and then at each other. Sweat beaded on their faces and trickled down their necks. Aurora's T-shirt was stained and sticking to her. And it had been eight hours since they'd seen anything resembling a crow.

She shrugged off the canvas bag and dropped it beside the rails. Polk broke into a grin. "Last one in is a rotten egg!"

Aurora tripped him, sending him sprawling on the embankment. She dashed for the pond, kicking off her shoes, jumping out of her jeans, and stripping down to her underwear. She danced out of her socks just in time to splash into the water. Polk stomped after her but stopped when he saw her jeans fly past him and land in the grass.

Aurora surfaced, gasping, delighting at the prickle of goosebumps. She looked around and saw Polk on the bank, staring at her with his mouth open.

"What?" she called. "Aren't you coming in?"

"You—" He gestured at her shirt and jeans lying on the bank.

"Don't be silly! I'm wearing underwear." But to her horror, she felt herself beginning to blush. "Well, I'm *sorry!*" She walked backwards deeper into the water until she was a head bobbing on top of its own reflection. "In our mad dash to escape, I somehow forgot to pack our swimsuits. Look, it's not like my underwear shows anything more. At least this way, you don't have to look the other way while I change into a bikini. Now, are you coming in, or what?"

Polk hesitated. Then he whooped and pulled off his pants, shoes and shirt. Aurora laughed. Polk dove into the water with a huge splash.

They swam lengths. Aurora took a few minutes to wash the mud, sweat and abandoned bathroom smell from her jeans and T-shirt, spreading them out to dry on the flowers. They spent the next half-hour splashing each other, playing tag, before finally collapsing by the water's edge, gazing up at the sky as the water lapped around them.

"We needed that," said Aurora at last.

"Yeah. We did." Polk sat up, sloshing water over her. "Let's eat."

She struggled to sit up. "Give me a hand here."

He clasped her hand. "Sure. Come on." He hauled her to her feet.

They slipped on the muddy bottom. Aurora teetered, her free arm cartwheeling. Polk staggered, but caught her, one hand clasped around her side. Aurora's breath caught. She'd never realized just how strong he was. They stood a moment, staring at each other, their faces dangerously close.

She saw Polk's gaze run quickly up and down her body, then plant itself at a safe spot somewhere by her right ear. His cheeks glowed red. To her disgust, she was blushing furiously too.

Polk coughed. "Um..."

"Don't let go yet!" she snapped. She was still balanced precariously on one foot, and Polk was taking her weight. She staggered fully upright. Then she cleared her throat and nodded curtly. "You can let go now. Thanks."

"You're welcome."

They turned their backs on each other and ran for their clothes.

Aurora felt more comfortable once she'd pulled on her jeans and shirt. They were stained and a bit damp but smelled okay. They worked together to sort out the canvas sack and hand each other water bottles. Sitting on the track embankment, they had a dinner of cold beans.

The sun set. The sky darkened, and the stars came out.

"So, I guess we're stopping here for the night?" Aurora rubbed the knots out of her legs.

"You want to wander around in the dark? Besides, we need our sleep."

"Yeah." Aurora lay back and looked up at the sky again and was startled at the number of stars she saw. The sky hardly had room enough for them all. "Wow," she breathed. "There really *is* a Milky Way."

She had spent almost three years in Cooper's Corners, but with a lifetime of experience that had already seen all the stars and grown tired of them. Now she looked up at them with the eyes of a city girl who hadn't realized that the sky had depth. The universe was a lot bigger than she'd ever thought it could be.

"What are we going to do, Polk?" she said at last.

He rolled over and clasped her hand. "Don't worry—"

"I'm not talking about this chase. I'm talking about after."

"Can't we just go back...to Matron?"

"No," said Aurora. "Not after keeping me there with my fake memories."

"Find your mother, maybe?"

"If I can." Then she shook her head. "But Mom abandoned me. I lived the rest of my life in a lie. Like it or not, I'm on my own." She rolled away from him and rested her head on her arm. "There's no going back. The only way forward is forward."

They lay in silence as the twilight deepened. Finally, Aurora rolled back over and looked at Polk. "Do *you* have any dreams?"

"Only when I'm dreaming."

"You're always dreaming," said Aurora.

He frowned at her.

"Seriously. Everybody dreams in the daytime, and not just in daydreams. You only notice your dreams when you're asleep, and your mind has nothing else to do. But the part of the mind that does the dreaming doesn't shut down. Everybody dreams, all the time."

Polk stared at her, eyebrows raised.

"Trust me," she said. "I know."

He gave her a lopsided grin. "If you say so."

He lingered on the grin, and she couldn't help blushing. The grassy embankment was bigger than all the beds in the world, but the thought of sharing it with him still gave her a strange thrill.

In her mind's eye, she slapped herself.

The moon rose. After a while, Aurora heard Polk snoring. She waited a moment longer, then scooched over on her back until her elbow touched his arm. She settled back with a contented sigh.

The wind brushes the wheat, rippling the tassels like surf.

Aurora blinked up at the sky. What had just happened?

She'd seen a dream. She'd seen Polk's dream, but she hadn't looked him in the eye.

Then she realized: this wasn't a dream at the back of his mind. This was what he was dreaming, right now. She'd picked it up like a radio.

She couldn't do that, could she?

Then again, until now, I've never slept next to anyone in my life. Who knows what the effect could be?

The images swept over her again.

His feet scrunch on the gravel. His breathing catches. Polk reaches out to part the first stalks of wheat.

Aurora sat up, her chest heaving. She looked at Polk's back, wondering if she should move away. She didn't want to leave him but this was...overwhelming, and far more intimate than she'd ever expected.

Is this my future, when I'm finally old enough to have serious relationships, to be battered by my lovers' dreams?

But as she hesitated, the images swept through her a third time, and she lost touch with the ground.

Polk walks through the wheat, his heart beating faster. He doesn't notice Aurora standing beside the path, staring at him as he passes.

Wait a minute, Aurora thought. She looked down at herself, at her arms. She pinched herself and raises a welt.

"What the hell?" she says.

Suddenly, Polk stands behind her. "What are you doing here?"

She whirls around. "I'm...sorry. I read dreams, remember?"

He breathes heavily. His cheeks are red. "A little privacy?"

"I'll just go." She stumbles towards Matron's diner.

"No!" Polk shouts. "Not that way!"

She opens the door, then stops, teetering, staring down into a pit.

The air fills with the screech of crows.

"Aurora!" Polk shouts, running to her, but too late. Aurora falls.

Sights and sounds bombard her. Memories.

...Polk slams through the diner door and tosses his schoolbooks aside. He turns to the stairs leading up to his room but stops to find Matron standing there.

"I've moved your stuff down here," she says.

He groans. "Aw, Matron!"

"She's here."

He stops mid-groan and looks into the living room. Aurora sits slouched on the battered couch, in her jeans and denim jacket. Her eyes are glazed, and she is flipping endlessly through the television channels on her remote.

"Go in and say hi," says Matron.

Polk stares at Aurora. He braces himself, then walks into the living room.

She takes no notice of him. He settles in beside her and can't stop staring. She gives him the briefest glance.

"Um...hi," he says.

"Hi," she replies, blandly, and flicks to the next channel.

He looks at her another moment longer, then smiles. He settles back into the sofa and watches television…

The air rushes past Aurora as she falls…

"Swear it!" Matron shouts. "Lives count on you, boy. Don't let your parents down."

"But I don't want to," Polk moans. "I don't know her. I don't know who she is. Why should I care?"

Matron stands up. She says nothing. But Polk looks at her, then takes a breath. "I swear to protect her. I swear…"

Aurora sinks further, lower…

…Matron is looking sad. Polk comes in and shows her the picture he's drawn, of her, cooking eggs on the grill. She smiles, then, and ruffles his hair…

Down she falls…

"Momma? Dadda?" Polk sobs.

Matron picks Polk up and hugs him to her shoulder. Her own shoulders quake. "I'm sorry, son. I'm so sorry!"

Further…

"It'll be nice to have a friend to play with, won't it?" says his mother.

Polk looks up from the toy train engine he's playing with. He grins.

"I don't think he's figured it out," says his father.

They sit in the corner of the hospital waiting room, near the box of toys. Others sit and read magazines, dimming the sunlight that shines through the window.

"Would they be related?" asks his mother.

"Distantly," said his father. "At most cousins, I think. I don't understand human family connections."

There is a commotion at the end of the corridor. The people in the waiting room look up, then stand up.

The dark man bursts in. Aurora gasps to see him. His eyes shine. "They say her water's broke. The baby is coming. I'm going to be a dad."

He grins. He looks down and sees Polk, and picks him up. "I'm going be a dad!"

"You be da," Polk mimics.

The dark man swings Polk around, carrying him across the hospital waiting room while Polk makes engine noises.

The dark man laughs. And Polk is laughing too. Laughing like a baby...

Aurora grunts as she hits bottom—

Polk rolled away, breaking the connection. Aurora was up on one elbow on the stubbled ground, her breathing ragged. She scrambled up and backed away from him, staring at his back and the moon shadow it cast.

Around her, the wind blew the smell of cold grass and loneliness. The land rolled away in moonlight. It was rugged, but at least she could see her way. Her legs were sore, but not so much she couldn't walk. And she didn't need to sleep. An hour or two was all she needed to make sure that he never found her.

She picked up the bag of water bottles, the cans and the can opener. After a moment's hesitation, she left two bottles behind Polk's back.

She cast one more glance at Polk's sleeping form.

"I'm sorry," she whispered. Then she turned away and set out away from the rail embankment, under the starry sky.

CHAPTER SIX:
SOLITUDE

THE MONDAY AFTER AURORA SAW ANNE'S dream, Aurora found herself in the cloakroom, hanging up her jacket beside Anne. The two girls looked at each other.

"Hey," said Aurora.

"Hey," said Anne.

They stood in silence.

"Look," said Anne. "I'm sorry."

Relief flooded into Aurora so hard it made her dizzy. "I'm sorry too!"

"It's just that...yeah, you're right, I'm jealous," said Anne. "Your mom can afford to get you all the good stuff, and my parents can barely get me a cake on my birthday. I just...I didn't think you could see it."

"I didn't," stammered Aurora. "It's...complicated."

"I like you," said Anne. "You're a good friend. I just wish—"

"I know," said Aurora.

They clasped hands. Without meaning to, Aurora looked Anne in the eye.

Laughter ripples through the classroom, rising in waves.

Aurora stands in everybody's sight, her presentation forgotten, eyes wide like a deer caught in the headlights.

Aurora's mouth opens and closes. Tears trickle down her cheeks. Even Miss Daultry is laughing.

Aurora snatched her hands from Anne's grasp. She backed away.

"What?" said Anne, blinking at her. "Aurora, what?"

Aurora turned away and stormed out of the cloakroom, leaving Anne behind.

At the door to the classroom, Aurora ran into an oncoming flurry of arms.

She recoiled, but Albijana caught her and wrapped her in a hug. Aurora stood, arms locked to her sides, as Albijana held her close.

"It worked!" Albijana squeezed tighter. "It worked!"

"What worked?"

"In my dream. When the planes came, I chose to fly. I found my dad, and we flew away."

The light dawned. "You did?" Aurora broke into a grin.

Albijana nodded vigorously. "I did! We flew over the ocean! We stood on clouds!"

Aurora hugged Albijana. "That's great!" Then she gently eased Albijana's arms away and stepped back. "That's wonderful!"

Albijana beamed. "Thank you!"

At the head of the classroom, Miss Daultry clapped her hands and called the class to attention. Albijana turned and headed for her desk.

As Aurora watched, she felt herself grinning like an idiot, even as Miss Daultry rebuked her for not getting to her desk quickly enough. She couldn't stop. Her heart felt suddenly and impossibly light.

I could use this, she thought.

I could use this.

❧

Aurora stepped carefully in the waning moonlight, alert for holes or sudden dips she could twist her ankle in. The grasses brushed her jeans. The wind made the only sound.

By the time the sky was starting to lighten, she was miles away from Polk. Rolling hills surrounded her. She might as well be the last person on Earth now.

When the sun peeked over her shoulder, brightening the landscape into ridges of flower and shadow, Aurora put it on her left and headed south. She was used to waiting tables. She was used to being on her feet all day. But her legs ached, and there was still far to go.

People can die in situations like this, she thought. *People* have died. *I'm crossing a wilderness on foot at the height of summer. Only an idiot would try this.*

Call me an idiot, then. What choice do I have?

The sun rose. Its heat pressed down on her back. The birds twittered. She hunched down, focusing on each step as she plodded forward. Step by step, she was getting closer to her goal.

Whatever that goal was.

The shadows grew shorter. The birds stopped twittering. Aurora's legs ached. Her head ached. She stopped and gulped down a bottle of water. She looked out at the rolling landscape and moaned.

A faint noise from behind her caught her attention. She looked around, but she was in a gigantic bowl and could see nothing. She listened hard. It came again.

"Aurora!" It was Polk's voice, at the top of his lungs, but at the very edge of her hearing. He was very far back. She couldn't see him. That meant he couldn't see her, either. She shouldered her canvas sack and wiped the sweat from her face. Taking a deep breath, she strode on faster.

Polk's cry echoed over the rolling landscape.

"No, Polk," she muttered. "Leave me alone."

"Why?" Anne fell into step beside her. "Why do you always want to be alone?"

Aurora stumbled. Anne caught her by the arm and steadied her. Aurora stared at her.

Anne looked years older than when Aurora had last seen her. Well, it had been years since she had last seen her.

"What are you doing here?!"

"Keeping you from talking to yourself, of course," said Anne. "You don't want to make people think you're crazy, do you?"

Aurora let out a short, sharp laugh and walked on. "Too late." She looked at her former best friend again. Anne wore a fuchsia crop top, dark jeans and shiny running shoes. The designer labels were tastefully prominent. "How did you afford all that stuff?"

"Got a job. Clothing store. Employee discount. They're the only good clothes I have."

"Mother still scrimping?"

Anne shrugged. "Yeah, but she's going to get me to college. What about you?" She ran her eyes up and down

Aurora. "You look like you haven't seen the inside of a Lululemon in years."

"I haven't. What's so bad about that? I'm working."

Anne chuckled.

"What's so funny?"

"It's just weird," Anne said. "We've swapped places, haven't we?"

Aurora scratched the back of her neck and smiled. "It's been an interesting, few years."

"Really?" Anne flicked an eyebrow. "Not if you spent it the way you spent the last weeks at school. You went off into your own world there. Wasn't it lonely?"

"Of course it was! You think I wanted this? Not being able to look anybody in the eye?" Aurora waved her hands, shaking the argument off. "This is stupid! You don't know any of this stuff! You're a figment of my imagination!"

"Or a hallucination brought about by thirst," said Anne. "Then again, maybe not. You read dreams, Aurora. You read *my* dreams. Do you think any explanation is going to make sense? Maybe *I'm* dreaming. Maybe you're reaching into my dreams, pulling me out to talk to you. Ever think of that?"

"Why would I do that?"

"Maybe you have questions?"

Aurora gave her a sideways look. "Do people miss me back home?"

Anne tilted her head. "We wondered where you went. There were a lot of rumours. But after a few weeks with no news, we moved on." She shrugged. "What did you expect? It's been, like, years!"

Aurora looked at her feet and kicked up dust as she walked. "I know."

"*I* missed you." Anne clasped Aurora's hand.

"Even after all I said to you?" asked Aurora.

"I'm sorry," said Anne. "I was jealous. I couldn't help that. But just because I was jealous didn't mean I didn't want to be your friend."

Aurora smiled. "Thanks."

They plodded along, Anne standing tall, Aurora bent nearly double by the weight of the sun and the canvas bag.

"How long have you been walking?" Anne asked.

"You sound like Polk," Aurora muttered.

"It's a simple question."

"Not long enough!"

"You're going to kill yourself if you don't rest."

"I can't," said Aurora.

"You have to—"

"I can't!" Aurora shouted. "If I lie down, I'll just stare at the sky and drive myself crazy. Don't you understand? I *don't* sleep. I haven't slept since I got my first period. It just doesn't happen."

Anne chuckled and shook her head. "And to think *I* was jealous of *you*." Her smile shifted to a frown. "You have to try."

Aurora grimaced as pain shot up her calves. "I'm on the run. I can't waste time trying to sleep—"

She stumbled on the uneven ground. Anne grabbed her, and a second set of hands helped haul her up.

Aurora blinked to find herself staring into Albijana's older, but still cheery, grin.

"You need rest," said Albijana. "You've been walking two days straight. What, you think you're Superman or something?"

"Are you two ganging up on me?" Aurora looked from one to the other blearily. She struggled to focus on the landscape ahead.

"Come on," said Albijana. "We'll keep the nightmares at bay. It's the least I can do."

Roger flashed into existence in front of them. Aurora flinched. Albijana scowled, and Roger vanished in a haze of heat.

"I don't—" Aurora began.

"Try," Anne and Albijana chorused.

"You can take our dreams," said Anne. "Maybe that's not the only thing you can borrow."

They pushed her up the hill and faded into the air behind her. Aurora reached the top and looked around.

The landscape spread out around her. It seemed to go on forever. And above her there was only sky.

She dropped to her knees and fell backward onto the wild grasses. She looked up at the blue dome and felt as though she were flying.

It was as though she had shrunk to the size of an ant or a microbe. She felt as though the blades of grass towered over her. She felt as if everything was around her, and yet she felt as if, in the whole universe, there was only her.

Even if she were naked, she couldn't have been more vulnerable, or more free.

"So, this is what it's like to dream." Her eyelids fluttered. "I'd forgotten."

And, for the first time she could remember, she voluntarily fell asleep.

A grass stalk tickled Aurora's face and she woke. Waking up felt weird, like surfacing from deep water. She sat up and shielded her eyes against the sunset. She looked around. Everything looked the way she had left it, but it all felt different. She felt refreshed. Her legs didn't ache, but there was more. The world spoke to her in crisp colour. The ground was ochre, the sky above a rich blue.

She stood and stretched, then took deep breaths of the cooling evening air. If this was what it was like to wake up, she felt a little sad to have missed out all these years. But she was ready to take on the world.

"Thanks, Anne," she muttered. "Thanks, Albijana."

She drank a bottle of water, pacing herself so she didn't chug it, and ate a breakfast (or was it dinner?) of cold beans. Then she picked up the bag. Keeping the sunset on her right, she walked on.

As she walked, she watched a thunderstorm drift north—not like the one in her dream at Matron's diner, but a single isolated storm, rising in the late day heat and marching across the rolling fields to the west, trailing a shadow of rain and lancing the ground with lightning. In the rolls of thunder, she felt her heart flutter and lift. She waved at the storm as it passed. An airplane passed overhead, the sound of its engines rising above the wind, and she shaded her eyes to watch it. She walked until half the sky was dark and the sun glowed red on the horizon.

She froze at a sound like a baby rattle. *I heard that before recently. Where?* She looked around and spotted movement. She turned. The head of a rattlesnake rose above the tall grass.

Another rattle behind her. And another to her left. Aurora turned some more. Eight rattlesnakes surrounded her, arranged like the points of a compass. Each was over a metre long, their patterned backs the colour of stone.

What the heck?

Aurora ducked back as a snake approached. She tried to run out of the circle, only to have the other snakes slither into her path. Their eyes followed her as she backed up to the centre of the circle. *This isn't natural. Were there ever any rattlesnakes around here? Isn't this too far north?*

It's another trap.

She scanned the horizon and spotted a figure coming towards her out of the northwest, a silhouette against the sunset. She glared, recognizing him before he called out to her.

"Hello, there!" Salvadore stopped outside the circle of snakes and stood with his hands clasped behind his back. "You look like you could use a little help! How fortunate that I just happened along—"

"Oh, cut the crap!"

Salvadore gave her a disappointed look. Then he drew himself up. "Come with me."

She folded her arms. "No!"

He took a deep breath and stepped forward. "Come with me...*please?*"

Aurora cocked her head. "You know, you might have considered asking me nicely, first, before you drugged me!"

He raised his eyebrows. "Would you really have come with me if I'd asked politely?"

"I'd have wanted to know why."

"Ah. Well, then. I'm sorry. I wouldn't have had the time to explain. I don't do well with questions that have complicated answers. Now, are you coming or not?" He gestured, and the snakes slithered towards her.

Aurora backed up. "How did you find me?" she snapped, desperate.

He grinned. "It wasn't hard when I found your trail, though you do move fast for such a little one. Don't you sleep?"

Aurora let out a laugh of disbelief. "You found me in mile after mile of Saskatchewan wilderness and then came right here, right away? I don't believe it! Where'd you even park?"

He shrugged. "I admit, I had a lucky break. We can travel fast if we need to. At the speed of dreams, you might say."

Aurora backed away from an advancing snake, but at Salvadore's words, she jerked up. "What did you say?"

"Surely, you've guessed this already! People like me—like us—play in the collective unconscious of the human mind. The dreamworld, you might say. All I needed was the subconscious thoughts of someone who had you in their line of sight to realize where you were and, with a bit of an effort, materialize."

"But I haven't seen anybody since—" Her mouth dropped open. "The airplane?"

"And there I was!" He winced and rubbed his back. "Bit of a hard landing. That's one reason we don't do that too often." He clasped his hands together. "Now, I know you're playing for time, so here's the deal: come with me and get a full explanation of what's going on. Don't and— oh, where did it go?" He patted his pockets and pulled out a vial and a syringe. "I inject you with this life-saving antivenom after these snakes…"

There was a flash of movement. Aurora yelled as a snake struck at her. She ducked away, tumbled, and suddenly the snakes were upon her, rattling. She flung up her hands. She heard the shift of air as the snakes struck— then a click as they hit…something. Then silence.

She opened her eyes, then looked up, heart pounding. The snakes surrounded her, staring down, jaws open, venom dripping, all leaning at an angle that suggested they were leaning on glass. They looked almost sheepish.

Aurora blinked. *Did I do that? How did I do that?*

She moved her hands, gestured and thought, *Get away from me.*

The snakes closed their mouths and slithered away, disappearing into the undergrowth. Aurora sat up.

Salvador cleared his throat. "That was…interesting. You're not as helpless as you look."

Nobody could be as helpless as I look, thought Aurora. But as the rattlesnakes vanished, she felt a surge of hope.

"Okay, then." Salvadore pocketed the vial and syringe. "New plan. You still want that explanation, right?"

Aurora shoved herself to her feet. She glared at Salvadore. "Who sent you?"

He nodded brightly. "Come with me, and I'll tell you."

"No. Tell me here, now!"

"I told you the answer's complicated. Do you really want to know, right now?"

"Of course I do!"

"Your father."

"What? No!"

Salvadore sighed. "See? I knew you wouldn't believe me. This is why I don't have these conversations just standing around outside."

"I never knew my father!" Aurora yelled "He was never around when I grew up. Never! Mom didn't talk about him. There aren't any pictures of him—"

He shook his head, smiling sadly. "Just because you've never seen your father doesn't mean he isn't looking for you. Why do you think your mother ran?"

Aurora gaped at him.

He smiled and reached out. "Come with me, and I will explain everything. Isn't it time you learned the truth?"

Aurora stared then took a tentative step forward. Suddenly, Matron's voice echoed in her head: *You can't let him take you, girl! It'll be disaster if he does!* She saw the funnel cloud of crows descending, heard the rifle going off…

She stepped back. "No."

Salvadore's glare darkened the sky, but Aurora stood firm. "No. I'm done. I'm sick of being hunted. I'm sick of being played with. I'm going to walk away, and nothing, and no one, is going to stop me."

Salvadore smirked. "You'll be leaving your boyfriend in the lurch."

Aurora's nostrils flared. "He's *not* my boyfriend!"

"Maybe not, but he certainly sees himself as your knight in shining armour," said Salvadore. "Fought valiantly, I must say. It'll hurt to realize you've abandoned him. Though I don't think the hurt will last much longer." He checked his watch. "Nope. Not much longer at all."

The colour drained from Aurora's cheeks. "What—?"

Salvadore ran at her, yelling. Without thinking, Aurora ducked aside, tripped him, and punched him on the back of his neck as he went down. She turned to run, then fell as he grabbed her ankle. She kicked, but he wouldn't let go. Her mind roiled as adrenaline kicked in.

I'm fighting for my life against a man who can control snakes! In a world where I'm attacked by my dreams.

Wait! I controlled the snakes, too, or blocked them. What if—?

She imagined snakes. She remembered them. She remembered a spring morning when she and Mom went north of Winnipeg to Narcisse where dens of garter snakes came out from hibernation. There were thousands of them. Tens of thousands. She shuddered at the memory. The ground had *seethed*.

As she remembered this, the ground dropped beneath Salvadore. He yelled as snakes slithered around him. He yelled louder when they slithered over him. Aurora struggled to scramble back, but his grip tightened on her ankle as he sank like in quicksand. "No!" he shouted, fear and shock in his voice. "No! Don't leave me!"

Aurora aimed her other foot and smashed his nose.

He let go. The garter snakes covered him, and he vanished underground. A hand reached desperately for the sky before sinking. The snakes sank too, until only grass and dirt remained.

Aurora sat up, gasping, staring at the sunken ground where Salvadore had been. She took a deep breath: "Holy sh—"

Her words caught in her throat. *What did he say about Polk?*

She scrambled to her feet. "Polk!" she shouted. "Polk!"

Aurora ran back the way she'd come.

☙

Aurora stumbled in the dying evening light. "Polk!" she shouted. "Polk!"

She kept running until she'd left Salvadore far behind, but she couldn't outrun the fear that gripped her chest. How was she going to find Polk in all of this emptiness?

She staggered to a stop. "Polk!"

Only the wind answered.

She beat her fists against her sides. *This isn't fair? If Polk dies because of me, I'll never forgive myself!* She ran her hand through her hair. *I can read people's dreams. That has to be good for something. There has to be some way to find Polk.* Has to be!

She lowered her hands. *Maybe there is a way. It's a long shot, but what choice do I have?*

She closed her eyes and took slow, deep breaths. Cleansing breath in, stressed air out. Cleansing breath in. She held it. *Thank you, Dr. Zane.* Another breath. *Where are you, Polk?*

She turned slowly and stopped when she felt a tug on her mind, a tug like north pulling the point of a compass. She took a step forward, then another. And another. The pull came stronger.

Aurora opened her eyes. She was facing roughly the way she'd come last night. There was nothing in front of her but more rolling hills, but she set off at a run. She ran until the twilight disappeared. She stumbled in the dark, drawn by that magnetic pull, until the moon rose in the southeast. She brushed past grasses and leafy saskatoon shrubs. Bullberry thorns snagged her jeans, but she pushed on. Finally, when she was almost out of breath, she reached a clearing, and the pull stopped. Aurora stopped. She staggered a little as she looked around.

"Polk?" she croaked.

She tripped on something at the edge of the clearing and fell full length. She sat up and looked, and her hand went to her mouth.

Polk lay tangled in the saskatoons. Their stalks and leaves wrapped around him, holding him half-upright, binding his legs and arms and twisting him into a painful, unnatural shape. More stalks had clamped over his mouth, while others had wrapped across his neck.

His eyes were closed. He wasn't breathing. As Aurora watched, the stalks tightened around his neck.

She scrambled forward. "No! Let him go! Let him go!" She grabbed and tore at the stalks. They held like rope and twisted in her fingers. Yelling, she clawed at the plant. Bits came free. Stalks snapped. Another branch swung at her, but she batted it away. She tore away the leaves and

attacked the stalks with her hands, her nails, her feet and
her teeth until the last stalk came free, and she pulled
Polk's limp body into the clearing. The plants stretched out
to grab her but drew back when they couldn't reach her.

Aurora crouched on her hands and knees, breathing
heavily. "Polk? Polk!" She slapped his cheeks, listened for a
breath, checked his pulse. She found it, weak and slow, and
sobbed with relief. He was still alive. But he wouldn't be
for long if he didn't start breathing.

She tilted his head back, opened his mouth and pinched
his nose. Placing her mouth over his, she breathed into
him. Out of the corner of her eye, she saw his chest rise.
She pulled back, then breathed into him again. And again.

On her fifth try, Polk coughed. His eyes fluttered open.
His voice was barely a whisper. "Are you doing the Prince
Charming role now?"

She laughed. Her eyes glistened and she cleared her
nose with a sniff. "You're okay!"

He beamed at her. Then his eyes widened, and he
rolled away suddenly, and lay, retching, his hands to his
throat. He wheezed. Aurora kept her hand on his back.
Polk collapsed on his stomach and breathed deep. Coughs
spasmed through him again. In between gasps, he said, "I
searched for you. Salvadore found me."

"I know. He found me too."

He looked up at her. "How…did you…get away?"

"He wanted to take me alive. That made it easier."

"Oh." Polk took several more gasping breaths. "Where
is he?"

She nodded over her shoulder. "Back there somewhere.

But we should get going." She got her hands under his arm and helped him stand.

He straightened up and looked at her. "Why did you run away?"

"Not now." Supporting his weight on her shoulder, she pulled him forward. "Where are the railway tracks?"

"This way," he wheezed. They shuffled forward to the edge of the clearing. Aurora flashed the plants a searing look, and they parted to let them pass.

Together, Aurora and Polk staggered into the night.

The next hours blurred as they stumbled across the moonlit prairie, scratching themselves on grasses and thorns. Polk was soon able to walk without Aurora's help, but she kept hold of his hand. He occasionally coughed or touched his throat. Aurora kept pace, but her mind tossed and turned.

"Who sent you?"

"You really want to know?"

"Yes!"

"Your father."

"What? No!"

"Just because you've never seen your father doesn't mean he's dead. Or that he isn't looking for you. Why do you think your mother ran?"

How could this monster who could call up crows, attack her in dreams, and hire snake-masters, be her father? It was incredible.

Her eyes focused on Polk, a wilting shadow in the

136

moonlight. *His dream showed me he'd known this crow-man who was after me. Awake, though, he's clearly not on that crow-man's side. Why is he protecting me?*

They reached the tracks with the moon overhead. They walked on south, rocks clacking beneath their feet as they stepped from tie to tie. Aurora hefted the bag over her shoulders and kept a close eye on Polk, who walked in a daze.

He's exhausted, she thought. *Why wouldn't he be? I slept through most of the day and haven't had plants strangle me.*

But it wasn't safe to stand still anymore. The tussle with Salvadore showed that the ones who were after her were no longer watching just the road. And given how Salvadore had found her, pointing to the airplane, that told her that once she got to Saskatoon, she'd be even easier to find.

So we have to keep moving. And there's no way Polk is going to be able to do that for much longer. And in this barren place, there are so few places to hide.

So, what the hell do I do? Pray?

I suppose it couldn't hurt.

Lord, get us out of this mess. Please.

Polk looked up. "What's that?"

Aurora looked. A pickup truck was parked on the rails of a track siding. Aurora frowned, then saw that the truck had been modified to run on the rails. The rubber wheels pushed it forward, but metal wheels in front and behind kept the truck on track. The logo of the railway was plastered on the truck doors, as they saw when they came up beside it.

Oh my. Aurora glanced up at the sky.

Polk tried the door handle on the truck's passenger side. It opened easily. The interior light went on.

"We're not going to steal somebody's ride," said Aurora.

"There's nobody around. Maybe they left it here and took a train home?"

Aurora scanned the horizon. There were no lights, no houses, no camp. "Are the keys in the ignition?"

Polk leaned into the cab. "Nope."

Aurora nodded. It couldn't have been *that* easy.

"I could hotwire it, though."

"What?" Aurora pulled him from the cab. "Where did you learn how to do that?"

He looked at her seriously. "From Joe and his gang. We were bored. We didn't have anything else to do."

"So, you stole cars?"

"I didn't!" snapped Polk. "I don't know about Joe. But...I think it was only his dad's car, and he put it back because there was nowhere else to go."

Aurora heaved a huge sigh. "God, I miss the big city."

Polk reached behind the steering wheel. (*A steering wheel?* thought Aurora. *On a* railroad?) He began pulling out wires. Two minutes later, the engine roared to life, and Aurora decided she would buy an anti-theft device for her first car.

But as Polk shifted over into the driver's side, Aurora reached through the window and tugged his sleeve. She pointed at the passenger seat. "You sit there. I'm driving."

"I can handle this—"

"Just get some rest, okay?" She tugged harder.

He sagged like a handful of wet noodles. Then he straightened up. "You promise not to run off?"

She smiled at him and crossed her heart.

He settled into the passenger seat and leaned back. Aurora came around the truck and slid into the driver's seat. The dashboard was similar to Matron's station wagon, with a set of railway-related computer equipment Aurora thought she could safely ignore. She pulled the truck into gear and pressed the accelerator. She reached for the steering wheel, then pulled back as the rails did the steering for her. There was a clatter underfoot as the siding merged with the mainline. The metal wheels sang as the truck picked up speed.

Polk began to snore. Images of his wheat field dream invaded her vision, but she pushed them away and concentrated on the drive.

"It'll be okay," she muttered. The headlights lit up a signpost beside the rails. It said SASKATOON: 200 KM. "It'll be okay. Matron told us to go to the city. She must have known what she was doing. Maybe the person she is sending us to can help us."

The rails sang beneath her and the ties rushing at her blurred.

It won't be long now.

CHAPTER SEVEN:
THE PARIS OF THE PRAIRIES

AURORA WALKED TO SCHOOL IN SILENCE, FOL-
lowing old routes on autopilot. Kids darted past,
laughing and calling to each other.

She passed through an alleyway between a store, a row
of houses and a park, a favourite shortcut for schoolkids
because it was out of the eyes of the teachers. She side-
stepped a group of kids kicking a ball about. Other kids
bounced balls off the back of the store.

Turning a corner, she saw Albijana stumbling backward
and landing heavily on the concrete. Roger and his stooges
laughed as Albijana rolled over, clutching her wrist.

As Roger stepped forward menacingly, Aurora darted in
front of him while Albijana struggled to her feet.

"What did you do that for?" Aurora yelled. "Leave her
alone!"

Roger stopped, startled. The moment stretched out,
then broke. He snickered. "Stay out of this, shorty. If you
know what's good for you."

He made a move to pass her, but Aurora planted herself
in his way. "Apologize!"

There was a gasp from the gathering crowd of children. Even Albijana caught her breath.

Roger rolled his eyes. "Get out of my way, squirt!" He tried to brush past her.

Aurora shoved him back with a grunt. Roger stumbled, more from surprise than from the shove. He scowled at her. "What the hell? You got a death wish?"

Aurora saw Anne at the back of the crowd, covering her mouth with both hands. Everyone stared at Aurora in shock or dread. Then a voice spoke up at the back of her mind: *I can use this.*

She trembled but kept her gaze steady. "I'm not afraid of you, Roger."

Roger grinned. "Oh, yeah?"

"Yeah."

"You wanna fight?" He laughed.

She kept her gaze locked on his face. She tried to slow her thumping heart. "Sure."

There was another gasp from the crowd. And a flash in his expression. For a moment— Aurora could hardly believe it was real—it was there: surprise, curiosity, even a hint of fear. This wasn't going the way Roger expected. Nobody had ever challenged him like this before. He clamped down on his doubts, and his glare hardened. He looked her in the eye. "Okay! Bring it on!"

As she looked into his eyes, she saw it.

Darkness. Fire. Roger screams.

Got you.

"Not right now." She ducked back as Roger swung at her.

"I knew it!" he shouted triumphantly. "You're chicken!"

"No," she said evenly. "School starts in five minutes. You want to explain to the principal how you were late because you were busy beating up a girl?" She held her voice steady. "After school. How about after sunset? Right here. All right?"

He sputtered. "Me? Sure!" He jabbed a finger at her face. "Just be here, you little twerp."

He pushed past her and stomped off.

Aurora let out a long breath. She wobbled, dizzy, then leaned against the wall for support.

The other children stared at her. Some remembered the time and nudged their friends. They left for school, many of them looking back.

Aurora found Albijana standing by her side, staring at her in wonder. "Why did you do that?"

Good question, said something in Aurora's mind. "I couldn't just stand there."

"He'll kill you!"

Yup, said that part of Aurora's mind. But she squeezed Albijana's hand. "Maybe. Maybe not. Will you help me?"

Albijana hesitated. She glanced after Roger and the others. Then she looked at Aurora and nodded.

Aurora smiled. "Good."

The song of the rails competed with Polk's snores. The signposts counted down the distance to Saskatoon. Aurora kept an eye on the way ahead, watching for, among other things, the light of an oncoming locomotive that would send them scrambling out of the rail truck. But as they drove on, she kept glancing over at Polk.

"Who are you, really?" she muttered.

I could wake him up and ask him point blank, confront him with the images of his dream. It's not like he'd skip out while we were driving at sixty kilometres per hour.

She was reaching out to nudge him when the car ran over a rail crossing next to a grain elevator. In the light of the loading ramp lamps, she saw him sprawled in his seat, mouth open, drooling, a vicious red mark across his throat.

Aurora pulled her hand back.

He's stayed with me through all this, she thought. *Even after I abandoned him. He may have hidden his true self from me after I confided in him my special powers, but when I ran away, he came after me. And got himself strangled by possessed saskatoon bushes.*

So, he's on my side. But what side am I on?

Ahead of her, the sky lightened towards dawn. *A new day.* Then she thought, *It's my birthday. I'm sixteen today.* In all the excitement, the date had sneaked up on her without her noticing.

She gave herself a wry smile in the rear-view mirror. *Happy birthday, Aurora!*

The truck ran over another level crossing. The flashing red lights of the crossing arms blurred as she passed. The hills had given way to farm fields. She scanned for crows, but the sky was empty.

Crows, she thought. *A man is hunting me who can control crows. He can trap me in dreams. He's powerful. How do I stop him?*

But I have powers, too. I can see people's dreams by looking them in the eye. I somehow called up snakes to suck Salvadore down into the dirt, and I found Polk. If this crow-man has all these extra powers I didn't know about, what other powers do I have that I don't know about?

She sat back in her seat and stared out the windshield. *How do you find extra senses you don't know you have? It's like exercising phantom muscles.*

She closed her eyes and took a deep breath. Then another. And another. She cleared her mind. Made it clean like a canvas ready for the painter.

Come to me.

She opened her eyes and looked at the brightening horizon. Her mouth dropped open. "Whoa!"

She applied the brakes, and the rail truck coasted to a stop. She threw it into park, left the engine running, got out and stood on the embankment.

They were atop a small rise. Below her, Saskatchewan stretched for miles beneath a dome of early-dawn blue. The silhouette of Saskatoon's skyline poked up at the horizon, its glow lightening the sky.

And in the fields, floating in five lines, each a mile apart, translucent curtains of shade slipped back and forth across the wheat, like thin bands of rain without the clouds.

They made no sound. Around her, only crickets chirped.

"What the hell?" she whispered.

But she knew, instinctively, what they were.

They're dreams! These are the things he trapped me with when I slipped in and out of the real world. And they're impossible to see by day.

The passenger side door opened. Gravel crunched

underfoot. "Aurora?" Polk said, still sleepy. "What's wrong?" He followed her gaze and took a step back. "Oh, hell!"

Aurora looked at him. "You can see them too?"

He turned to her, opened his mouth to answer, and then froze. She could see the wheels turning.

"You've just given yourself away."

Polk groaned. "I'm an idiot!" He beat his hands against his sides. He kicked the side of the truck. He turned away and thumped the door with clenched fists. Then he looked at her. "You knew I was hiding something, didn't you?"

"When you fell asleep last night, I overheard one of your dreams. I knew you had something to do with that crow-man who's following us."

Polk shook his head. "That's why you ran away. You thought I'd betray you? After I walked across the wilderness with you? Through the heat, carrying that stupid canvas bag?" His voice rose. "Eating cold *beans*? Running after you and getting strangled by plants?" He pounded the roof. "How could you think that I would ever—"

"Then who are you, Polk?" she yelled. "*What* are you?"

"I'm not a monster or some alien. I'm just like you."

"If you're *just* like me, then I wouldn't be too sure about the not-a-monster part!"

His breath caught. He stared at her. "You're *not* a monster, either," he said softly.

"Then *what* am I?"

He looked away. "I don't know."

Aurora swore.

"I mean, I don't know how to describe it. It's just that...

we're different. We don't really belong where we are, but we have nowhere else to go."

"Who are 'we'?"

Polk waved his arms. "You. Me. Matron. Us. We look human. I feel human. My mom was human, but I'm... not. Well, not completely. We..." He sighed. "We normally inhabit the realm of dreams."

Aurora tasted this on her tongue. "Realm of dreams?" she echoed.

"Well, we're not there now. We've scattered across Earth, trying to live like normal people."

She let out a short, sharp laugh. "Good luck." She looked up at him. "Why scattered?"

Polk looked at the curtains of shadow shifting back and forth in front of the sunrise.

"Because of the man in black? Who is he, Polk?"

His face was grim. "He's the king."

"The king of what?"

"Of dreams."

Aurora snorted in disbelief. "The king of dreams? I'm being hunted by the dream king?"

Polk nodded.

"What's going on, Polk?"

He rubbed his forehead. "Look, do you think we could talk about this while we're driving? We're wasting gas just standing here."

She looked at him a long moment, then opened the door. They climbed inside. Aurora put the truck in gear. It sped up, and the ties between the rails became a blur again. She eased back in her seat and looked at Polk, her arms folded across her chest. He sat hunched up on the passenger's side, staring at his knees, his knuckles pressed to his lips. Finally, he spoke.

"I did swear to protect you. Three years ago, when Matron told me you were coming, she told me you were in danger and that the Dream King would try to find you. She told me it was very important that this didn't happen. She made me swear on the memory of my parents."

"That's a lot to dump on a kid."

"I could handle it," Polk said carelessly, still not looking at her. "I don't remember much...But I do know the Dream King killed my parents."

Aurora sat up in her seat.

"My father was...one of us," he said. "My mother was a nurse, I think. I was just a little kid when it happened, so I don't remember everything. Matron took me in."

She had to clear her throat. "I'm sorry."

"It's okay. It was years ago."

"How did the Dream King kill your parents?"

He flinched. "I don't know! Nobody knows for sure. It was like there was an explosion and then a great big fight to get him back under control. Then we scattered."

"Why?"

"The dream realm wasn't safe for us anymore, Matron said. Not with him...hunting."

They scattered, like my mom, Aurora thought. *That wasn't Winnipeg I saw in my mother's dream three years ago. And she's been a school counsellor for as long as I can remember, not some fancy psychologist.*

Then, is it true? Is the Dream King really my father?

Matron's words echoed in her head. *You can't let him take you! It will be disaster if he does!* Followed by Polk's *hunting.*

I don't want a dad like that.

They drove on in silence for several minutes. Finally, she asked, "Why are you doing this, Polk? Protecting me?"

"I told you, I swore—"

"On your parents' grave, who you never really knew," she cut in. "That's not a good enough reason to follow me across this wilderness. So why are you really here?"

He closed his eyes. "Don't ask me that. Please."

"Tell me."

"It's not important."

"Tell me!"

"Fine!" he shouted, rounding on her. "Look at me."

She looked him in the eye.

Polk walks across the gravel lot behind the diner and pushes aside the stalks of wheat as he enters the neighbouring field. He smiles as he wades into the waving sea of golden brown. The blue skies stretch on forever, and he shields his face from the sun.

The familiarity of Polk's dream swept over her. She lost herself in the images, momentarily drinking in the security and comfort she'd known before everything went to hell.

Polk wades through the wheat. His heartbeat speeds up as he slips through the stalks towards the clearing where they'd arranged to meet.

Wait, thought Aurora. *I haven't seen this bit before.*

There is Aurora, luminous, beaming at him, reaching out to him. Polk takes her hand. She wraps her arms around him. They kiss. They—

Oh!

Huh.

Um…

Aurora stared at Polk. Polk looked away. "Happy now?"

"Uh." Aurora faced front and twisted her hands together. "Yeah…uh…no…uh… How long…?"

"Since I first saw you." Polk sank into his seat. His glare could have burned a hole in the dashboard. "I thought—I *think*—that you are very beautiful."

She looked at him in astonishment. He glanced out the front window. "Now I think you'd better stop the truck."

Aurora snapped her attention back to the windshield. She jammed on the brakes. The rail truck skidded to a stop. A towering shade slipped silently up the rail embankment and over the rails in front of them, slow as a battleship in harbour. The rising sunlight shone through it as though it were gauze. It was hundreds of feet long, its top lost in the sky. She wondered whose dream it was or if it was a collection of dreams. Either way, she knew she didn't want to get caught in it.

"Okay," she breathed. "Just hold still…"

Polk held his breath.

A gap between the curtains crept across the landscape towards them. It looked barely wider than the truck. Aurora put the car in gear but kept her foot on the brake. As the gap eased itself up the rail embankment, she jammed on the accelerator. The truck shot forward. The gap slipped in front of them, and they sped through, with only inches to spare. The curtain of shade filled the rearview mirror. Aurora breathed again.

The next line of shades was a mile down the track. The rail truck paused until a gap passed in front of them, then they zipped through. They stopped and started through the two lines of shades that came next. The sky brightened, and the silhouette of Saskatoon's skyline drew nearer.

The sky was pale green and peach with dawn by the time Aurora brought the rail truck to a stop in front of the last line of shades. They sat a long moment, engine idling, while Aurora peered out the front window. "These are getting harder to see in daylight."

Polk leaned forward, squinting. "Yeah. This is going to be a problem."

"Help me, Polk."

He looked at her. "How? What makes you think I can help you?"

"I only just realized I can see these things. You saw them right away. I can only see...like...super-thin bedsheets. They're like ripples of air."

"That's about what I can see, too, yeah."

"I need you to tell me when I can go."

They looked at each other. Polk faced forward. "Okay. Get ready."

Aurora strained to focus on the next gap in the final line of shades. The edges of the dark sheets looked ragged, as though sunlight had chewed through them. Keeping one foot on the brake, the rail truck in neutral, Aurora revved the engine.

"Now!" Polk snapped.

Aurora shoved the truck into gear and stamped on the accelerator. The truck shot forward. Suddenly, the vague patch of shadow in front of them solidified into a curtain that was directly across the railway tracks. Aurora gasped, but before she could hit the brake, the edge of the curtain came into view in front of her. The tracks were clear. The car sped through.

She glanced at the rear-view mirror, and her breath caught. The wind of their wake had plucked at the shade curtain, and it was fluttering up, after them. The veil of darkness descended on the truck. Around her, Aurora heard the distant cry of crows.

Aurora pushed the gas as hard as she could. The truck sped up. The curtain floated down, brushing over the tailgate before settling back on the tracks. It drifted slowly across the fields, then vanished in a beam of sunlight.

Aurora looked at Polk and grinned. "Thanks!"

"Don't mention it." He looked away.

Aurora stared at him, but he didn't look back, so she faced forward. The rail truck drove on toward Saskatoon.

They saw their first cars as they approached the city. A highway swung into view and paralleled the railway tracks. Aurora turned her head to watch the vehicles; it felt like days since she'd seen people in cars.

She stopped the truck at a crossing with a gravel lane leading off the highway. Ahead of them, they could see the skyline of the city.

"Here we are," Aurora said. "Saskatoon."

"The Paris of the prairies," said Polk. "Well, what do we do now? Get out and walk?"

Aurora pulled out the paper Matron had thrust at her before she fled Cooper's Corners. The slip was torn, and water and sweat had made the ink run, but she could just make out what Matron had written. She pocketed it. "We could spend hours wandering through this city on foot. No, we've got to keep driving."

"Okay, but in what?"

Aurora looked at the rail truck dashboard and spotted a lever with an image of a set of railway tracks on it. She flipped it up. Machinery whirred underfoot as the metal wheels retracted. Then she pressed the accelerator and turned the steering wheel. The truck swung onto the gravel lane, bumping over and off the rails, and stopped by the side of the highway. They waited for a gap in the traffic, then drove down the road into the city. Aurora felt the traffic close around her like a blanket.

"Okay," said Polk. "When I can afford a car, I'm buying one of these."

Aurora chuckled. "As if."

They followed the highway into the city. Aurora kept her eyes open for crows, strange clouds, or Salvadore standing on a street corner.

Then again, if what he said was true and he could appear a few feet away from somebody by way of their dreams, she could understand why he wouldn't use that power often. If he appeared here in traffic in front of her car, she'd probably dent the truck. Twice.

After a couple of wrong turns, they found the address in a shopping plaza tucked among a field of box stores, and they swung off the road into the parking lot.

They stood at the edge of a patch of empty asphalt, buffeted by the sounds of traffic. A building stretched around two sides of the lot, filled with small stores that were still dark beneath a canopy that covered the walkway in front of them. Only the breakfast bakery at the end of the row of stores was open. In the breeze, Aurora caught the heady smell of bread baking. Her stomach rumbled. She looked at Polk and caught him staring wistfully at the bakery.

She touched his arm. "Let's find this place first. Then we'll eat."

His face fell, but he nodded and followed her across the parking lot. They looked for Unit D, found the fourth shop from the end of the row and tried the door. It was locked.

Polk stood behind her and peered at the items on display in the window. "Huh." There were books about fairies and a glass dish of crystals and semi-precious stones.

Aurora looked up at the sign. "'Mystic Dreamers'? Why would Matron send me to some New Age shop?"

She stopped when she saw a glass spirit ball dangling from the top of the door on the other side. She felt a feeling of familiarity, like déjà vu.

"Matron didn't say who she was sending you to?" Polk asked.

"There wasn't time."

"So, what do we do? Wait?"

Aurora ran her hand over the door and touched the glass in front of the spirit ball. "I guess. Maybe we could have a little breakfast—"

"Aurora?" The tone of Polk's voice made her look up. He nodded over her shoulder. "Someone's watching us."

Aurora turned and saw a woman standing at the end of the covered sidewalk, framed in the early morning light. Aurora's eyes widened, and her mouth dropped open.

The woman stood with her arms limp at her sides, a bag of groceries forgotten where it had fallen on the ground, oranges rolling away across the parking lot and beneath parked cars.

She looked smaller and thinner than Aurora remembered. Her smart pantsuit had been replaced by a floral dress and a beige windbreaker, and her blonde hair was longer and wilder. She looked pale without makeup, as if she'd been bleached by the sun and hollowed out by the wind.

A lump caught in Aurora's throat. She cleared it away. "Mom?"

Dawn Perrault's hands rose to cover her mouth. She dropped them and took a step forward, then another, and another. Soon, she was running. The air left Aurora's lungs as her mother threw her arms around her. Polk dodged out of her way. Aurora staggered back into a support column with a grunt.

"It's you!" her mother gasped. "It's really you! I thought I'd never see you again."

"Mom," Aurora gasped. Even Dawn's hair seemed thinner, brittle, like it could break in Aurora's fingers.

"Look at you!" Dawn cupped Aurora's face in her hands. "You've grown up! You're a young woman! I've missed so much."

"Mom!" Aurora struggled to free herself.

"What are you doing here?" Dawn was babbling.

"How did you know how to find me?" She stopped. "Does Matron know?" Her eyes scanned the parking lot as though checking for hiding places.

"She sent us here. She said I could be safe here."

"What? How?" Dawn's gaze fell on Polk. Her eyes narrowed. "And you are?"

Polk flushed red and gave a little wave. "I'm Polk, Matron's foster son. Pleased to meet—"

Dawn suddenly whipped out her purse and fumbled through it. "C'mon, we can't stand out here. Inside!" She yanked out her keys with a spray of Tic Tacs and used Kleenex, unlocked the door and swung it open. "Inside! Now!"

An electronic doorbell tweedled as Aurora and Polk crossed the threshold. Aurora coughed at the rush of incense. Wickerwork and sackcloth muffled the traffic noise outside. The shelves held bowls of beads, carved wooden toys and bags of Fair-Trade coffee. The counter was improvised out of milk crates and a single plank of wood.

Aurora looked up. The ceiling was festooned with spirit balls.

Dawn began to flutter about, moving papers off the counter and rearranging the bowls on the shelf. "Excuse the mess. Have you come a long way?" She gave them a quick glance. "Yes, of course you have. You must be hungry, but I don't think I have anything to eat."

Aurora stood in the aisle, surrounded by crystals and beads. Polk stood behind her. "Mom."

"Maybe we could grab a bite at the bakery," her mother went on. "They do a decent egg sandwich—"

"Mom!" Aurora cut in.

Dawn stopped. She looked at her daughter, her shoulders trembling.

There was so much Aurora wanted to say, so many questions, that the words caught in her throat. She looked around at the shadowy store, the improvised counter and the battered cash register. "You...you own a shop?"

"It pays the bills."

Silence descended. Mother and daughter stared at each other across the counter.

"Mom." Aurora's fists clenched and unclenched. "Why didn't you tell me?"

Dawn shook her head. "You were twelve, Aurora."

"Right! I was twelve. Do you know how frightening it is to have something like this happen to you when you're twelve? Do you know how frightening it is to think you're alone?"

"Yes, I know how frightening it is to be alone, Aurora."

"You knew!" Aurora yelled. "You could have told me—"

"I didn't know *what* to tell you!" Dawn shouted. "All I knew was that it wasn't safe for you anymore."

"So, you wiped my memories? You sent me away to hide with Aunt Matron? Some plan, Mom! Guess what: it didn't work!"

The colour drained from Dawn's face. "He came for you?"

"Yeah. Who is he, Mom? Is he really my dad?"

Dawn turned away and covered her face with her hands. Aurora stood, breathing heavily.

Dawn turned back, wiping her cheeks. Leaning on the counter for support, she looked Aurora in the eye.

156

Dawn steps forward. "Show me."

The Dream King's smile widens. He opens the door of his truck.

Dawn climbs in.

The truck drives out of the parking lot and onto the road, heading into the night. Faster it moves, and faster, breaking speed limits, but no one notices. The streetlights play off its shiny black exterior, fluttering off the mirrors, teasing the shadows like feathers. The wheels lift off. Wings catch the air.

The giant crow rises skyward, Dawn clasping the back of its neck. She smiles...

Aurora shook herself from the dream.

Dawn touched her wrist. "I'm sorry, honey. I'm so sorry. Look, let's...let's have some breakfast, okay? I'll think better if I have some coffee inside me. Then I can tell you everything I know. Please, Aurora?"

Aurora looked at her hands, then nodded.

"You two go on to the bakery," said Dawn. "I've got to write a note for the door: 'Back in 30 minutes' or something."

"Promise you won't run off?" Aurora said in a small voice.

Dawn crossed her heart.

"C'mon Polk." Aurora walked out the shop door. Polk grinned nervously at Dawn, who glared at him, then followed.

As they strode along the sidewalk towards the bakery, Aurora said, "You don't have to be here for this, Polk."

"Uh, yes, I do," he said reluctantly.

"There's going to be a lot of tears."

"Maybe I could go to the back or something. Seriously, are you okay?"

"Sure, I...well...now that I'm so close to the truth, I—this scares me."

The air darkened as though a cloud had passed in front of the sun. As they reached the bakery, Polk frowned at the bright blue sky and pushed open the door. The shop bell jangled as they entered. Aurora and Polk took deep breaths of air scented with fresh-baked bread. Then they looked up and saw that this ceiling was also hung with spirit balls.

"Mom's doing good business," Aurora muttered.

"Hmm?" said Polk. Aurora gestured at the ceiling. He looked. His brow furrowed. "What's the deal with these?"

"They're...charms," said Aurora. "Harmless stuff to keep glassblowers employed and less culturally appropriative than dreamcatchers. They're supposed to trap bad dreams."

Polk raised an eyebrow, then looked up at the spirit balls again. "She likes to be prepared. Protecting her store *and* her favourite coffee shop."

"Hey," said a waitress standing by the counter. "Have a seat!" She waved at a table by the front window. The restaurant was more than half-full of factory workers or older couples, all eating breakfast.

Polk and Aurora sat. The waitress was by their side instantly. "Hi!" she chirped. "What can I get you?"

"Coffee," Aurora said.

Polk nodded. "Coffee."

The waitress flipped up her notebook and began scribbling. "And the breakfast special today is three eggs, any

158

style, with your choice of bacon, sausage or ham, with hashbrowns and toast, just $9.95. Does that sound good?”

“Sure,” said Aurora. “Scrambled. Sausage. Brown toast.” She looked at Polk. “You?”

“The same.”

“Thank you!” the waitress chirped. “I’ll be right back.” She fluttered off.

Aurora watched her go. “I’m not ever like that, am I?”

“Only if you accidentally put sugar in your coffee.” Polk gave her a lopsided grin, and Aurora smiled to see it. She realized then that she didn’t want to lose it.

She leaned forward and clasped his hand. “Look, I’m sorry. I should have trusted you.”

“It’s okay.” He looked at his hand in hers. “Somebody should have told you. This would have gone a lot easier if there were fewer secrets.”

“You’re not kidding...”

“But nobody has all the answers, Aurora,” said Polk. “They probably never will. You’d better be prepared for that.”

“The Dream King might know,” she said under her breath.

Polk stared at her as if he hadn’t heard her properly. “Aurora, don’t think that. You don’t want to be anywhere near him. It’ll be a disaster.”

“Yeah, well, how do you know that? Did you see what happened? Can you explain it? I have a feeling that I’ll only stop running once I get all the answers.”

Polk looked out the glass door. “Here comes your mom. Let’s see what she tells you.”

The shop bell jangled. Dawn paused at the threshold, taking a deep breath. Then she crossed the floor and sat down across from them.

The waitress came sweeping in, plunking mugs of coffee on the table. "Here you go! And would the lady like anything?" She held her notepad at the ready.

"Nothing for me, thanks," said Dawn. "Just coffee."

"Sure!" the waitress chirped. Dawn waited until the waitress was away, then leaned forward. "Aurora—"

The waitress came bustling back and plunked the coffee down in front of Dawn. "Oh, I almost forgot," she said to Aurora and Polk. "We're out of sausages. Bacon or ham only for the special today."

"Bacon's fine," said Polk.

"Me, too," said Aurora through her teeth. "Thank you."

"Great!" The waitress beamed and whisked away. Dawn, Polk and Aurora looked at each other. Silence stretched.

Dawn took a deep breath. "Aurora—"

"Shall I top up your coffee?" The waitress was right beside them, holding the carafe expectantly.

The three glared at her. Dawn turned to Aurora and said, "What do you want to know about your father?"

The waitress looked from Aurora to Dawn and back again. "Oh, is this a bad time?"

Aurora and Dawn glared at her again.

The waitress laughed nervously. "I'll come back later, then."

Dawn turned back to Aurora and continued more quietly. "Love, ask me anything. You deserve to know. I'll tell you all I can."

"Who is he, Mom?" asked Aurora. "Is he really my dad?"

Dawn steepled her fingers over her mouth and nose and sat still for a long moment. Then she looked Aurora in the eye.

"Before you were born," she began. "I ran a successful practice as a psychologist in Toronto. I specialized in hypnosis and the dream state."

"Now close your eyes, Sally, and tell me what you see."

"I'm flying, Dr. Perrault," says the child. "I'm flying over mountains."

"I dealt with night terrors," Dawn went on. "I was good at what I did."

"Where are you flying to?"

The child breathes deeply. "Nowhere. It's so beautiful. I don't want to come back down."

Then the girl's brow tightens. "But something is pulling me down."

Dawn frowns.

"No," Sally whimpers. "It's dark!"

"But there was one particularly tough case," said Dawn. "A girl named Sally." She looked Aurora in the eye again. "Nothing would make her nightmares go away."

Aurora slips into Dawn's dream. She stares through Dawn's eyes at Sally, the little, brown-haired girl, sitting in a chair, her eyes closed.

Sally opens her eyes, and Aurora slips further in.

Dreams into dreams.

Sally stands in the middle of a forest. Aurora stands beside her, but Sally doesn't see her. The air breathes whispers. Sally sees faces at the edge of her vision, faces which disappear each time she looks at them. She hears the rustle of feet and paws approaching.

"Stay away!" Sally yells. "Stay away!"

Dawn's voice echoes from around the dreamworld. "You know what to do, Sally. It's your dream. Use it!"

Sally closes her eyes. When she looks around again, a wall is growing around her, brick by brick, rising up and closing above her head.

Dark leafy hands slam against the window. The oak door shudders against the beat of something heavy outside.

"It's not working!" Sally wails. "They're coming in!"

The door cracks, bulges.

Sally screams. Aurora rushes forward to hug the girl, but her arms pass through Sally's body.

Dawn's clinical voice echoes around them. "Sally, it's only a dream. You are in control. Find your strength, Sally. You need to find your strength."

"But suddenly, I had a breakthrough," said Dawn in the coffee shop.

Sally stops, then looks up at Aurora. "Who are you?"

Aurora starts to answer, but realizes that Sally is not looking at her, but through her.

She turns around and sees the Dream King.

Aurora gasps and crabwalks back, but he doesn't look at her. He is a mass of shadow. He has dark hair and is wearing black jeans, black boots and a black shirt with a collar. Behind him stands Matron, smiling approvingly.

The Dream King gently lays a hand on Sally's shoulder.

Dawn's voice echoes. "Sally? What's going on? Who is with you?"

The man smiles at Sally, like the sun behind clouds.

"Who are you?" Sally asks again.

"Strength," he says, with a voice like thunder.

He kneels behind Sally and takes her hand, holding it out. The air shimmers in front of her fingers, and the walls distort in front of them, like clay beneath a sculptor's hand.

Sally focuses on her fingers, and the world changes.

The door dissolves, leaving only sunshine and meadow behind. Somewhere in the distance, a dark shape screams its frustration. The sound fades.

Sally stands with the dark man in the world she created, on a top of a hill, overlooking a meadow.

"Fly," says the dark man.

And Sally flies.

Aurora blinked out of the dream. She rubbed her forehead and kept her gaze on the table.

"It was a miraculous recovery," said Dawn. "I've never had anything as good. I counted it up as luck, but that night...he appeared."

Aurora remembered her mother's dream.

"I have been wanting to meet you for a long time, Dawn. I've seen how you heal people's dreams. You're a Dreamwalker. I've watched your gentle hands at work—"

"I'm a psychologist. A hypnotist. I don't use my hands."

He laughs. "Will you come with me?"

She steps forward. "Show me."

He opens the door of his truck. Dawn climbs in...

"You met him that night." Aurora looked up at her mother in disbelief. "And you just went with him? You didn't know a thing about him!"

Dawn's eyes flashed with defiance. "I know it wasn't rational, but I don't regret it. I don't regret it at all. I have never loved anyone or have been loved in the way that he loved me."

Aurora shifted uncomfortably.

"It wasn't long before I was pregnant." Dawn looked down. "I never once thought about having a child until I was with him. And he stayed with me. We looked forward to our lives together, raising you." Her eyes darkened. "But it didn't work out that way."

"You ran," said Aurora. "Why?"

Dawn grabbed a napkin. She twisted it in her hands. "I had to. Something terrible happened."

"Mom, what happened the night I was born?" asked Aurora. "Why are we running?"

Dawn's breathing quickened. "Bad things. I don't *want* to remember!"

The waitress was at their table again. "Will you be having any dessert?" she squawked.

Aurora waved her away. "Not now, we're—"

Wait a minute. Squawked?

Aurora looked up. The waitress cocked her head. She looked at Aurora from first one eye and then the other.

Aurora stood up, knocking her chair back. Dawn screamed.

The waitress tucked her notepad under her arm. "The Dream King will see you now."

Then she flung out her arms. Above them, the spirit balls exploded. There was a flurry of feathers and glass shards. Aurora flung up her hands to protect her eyes.

When she opened them again, the door of the restaurant swung open to the jangle of the shop bell, and the waitress was gone.

Aurora and Polk stared around at a restaurant that was full of statues.

Outside, Saskatoon stood silent and motionless.

CHAPTER EIGHT:
BOUNCING OFF CLOUDS

ALBIJANA HUNG BACK AS AURORA LOOKED UP AT the buildings that lined the alleyway. They were blank walls of brick, with only one window breaking the monotony. Two lamps near the window winked on in the early twilight.

"Why are you doing this?" Albijana asked.

"Somebody has to teach Roger a lesson," said Aurora.

"Teach him what? How to hit a moving target?"

Aurora smiled at her. "It will be okay. Trust me."

Albijana looked at her a long moment. "What do you need me to do?"

Aurora handed her a couple of pairs of large black athletic socks. She pointed at the lamps. "I want this alleyway to be a bit darker. I'm not a good climber. Can you climb up there and pull these over the lights?"

Albijana took the socks, looked at the lamps, then looked back at Aurora. "Okay."

As Albijana climbed up the posts and dragged socks over each lamp. Aurora looked around as the shadows deepened and the alleyway dimmed to twilight.

Finally, Albijana slipped back down to the pavement. "What now?"

"We wait, and you stay out of the way."

"That's all? What are you going to do? Why do you want it to be darker?"

Aurora just smiled. "You'll see." *At least, I hope we'll see.*

They heard footsteps, the scuff of sneakers. They weren't alone anymore. Other kids had begun to cluster around trees and fence posts, straining to get a good look without getting in the way. The alleyway filled with mutters and giggles. Aurora touched the flashlight she had hidden up her sleeve. "It's almost time."

"Aurora," said Albijana. "We can still run. You don't have to do this."

"No. No more running."

The giggles stopped.

Roger sauntered into the alleyway.

✹

Aurora and Polk stood in the middle of the silent bakery. Their shoes crunched on broken glass as they shifted. Nothing else moved. The customers looked like three-dimensional photographs. Aurora turned to Dawn. "Mom!"

Dawn was frozen. Then she started to fade and so did the other customers, vanishing like ghosts until Polk and Aurora were alone.

Outside, in the clear blue sky, thunder rumbled.

"He's got us," Polk whispered. "I should have known—when the sun dimmed, there weren't any clouds. Before we came in here, remember? It was a dream curtain."

Aurora shushed him. Polk's voice seemed impossibly loud in the silence. She thought she could hear her thumping heart. She strode out of the bakery and into the parking lot. The stores were all closed, even her mother's. Aurora tried the door and stared at the darkened window, feeling a pang of loss. She'd only just found her mom again.

The few parked cars were empty. In the roadway next to the parking lot, cars stood in traffic, empty, their headlights on. "What's he done to all the people?"

Polk pinched his wrist. "Ow!" He pinched it again. "Ow! Oh, this is bad!"

Aurora swallowed the panic building in her throat. She ignored the traffic lights and crossed the road. Polk followed her. The stoplights changed. The clicking of the switches in the lamppost sounded loud in the silence.

Halfway across the road, Aurora turned and walked along the yellow line that ran down the centre. The wind whistled through the telephone wires.

She stopped. Polk stopped beside her.

"This city's empty," Aurora said

"You think?" Polk said sarcastically.

"Except for us."

Thunder rumbled again. Aurora looked up and around. When she looked north, she flinched. The sky above was clear and bright, but the northern sky was dark. Clouds billowed onward like weather in a sped-up film. Lightning flickered over the buildings.

She swore and began walking again.

If you're looking for someone, she thought, *one way to find them is to remove everyone who isn't that someone. The person that's left is the one you want.*

She watched the pouring clouds. *Even in dreams, what could make a whole city's population disappear, even the dogs? Heck, what if it isn't just this city? What if me and Polk are the only two humans left on the planet?*

A thing like that could squash me like a mosquito if it wanted to. So, why didn't it?

But if this thing is my father, he wouldn't want to squash me, would he? He'd want to hug me and hold me, kiss my scrapes and make it all better. He'd want to hurt those who'd taken me away from him. He'd tear the human race apart to find me.

And that's just what he's done.

But this can't be my father, she thought. *There's no way I could be related to* that!

"Aurora!" said a voice like thunder.

The voice came from everywhere at once, echoing off walls and hills, bouncing around buildings. Now Polk and Aurora were surrounded by warehouses and factories that blocked the view of the horizon. Aurora looked around for a better vantage point. She spotted a ladder bolted to side of a long, squat building, the sign on which advertised "5 Pin Bowlerama." The ladder led to the roof. She ran over and clambered up the metal rungs, Polk close behind her.

They stepped out onto the gravel-covered roof. The northern sky stretched out above, black and boiling.

"Aurora!" The voice made the roof shake.

"Where's the voice coming from?" She looked around but saw nothing. Polk looked at the sky. He leaped back in shock. "Sweet Jesus!"

Aurora looked at the northern horizon.

The northern horizon looked back at her.

A trick, Aurora told herself, a slant of the early morning sunlight that turned the clouds shiny white or night black. Shadings formed eyes, nose, lips, in the shape of the man who had come to the diner, all in black, right down to his eyeballs.

Except that the cloudy lips moved. "Aurora. I have found you at last."

"Who...are you?"

The face smiled. "I am the Dream King."

Gravel scrunched behind her as Polk slipped back against the wall of a utility hut.

Aurora clenched her fists. Her heartbeat pounded in her ears. She licked her lips. "Why have you been chasing me?"

"Don't you know me, Aurora? I am your father."

Aurora stared at the cloud face, her hands clenched at her sides, searching for something familiar, either from distant memory, or from her own gaze into a mirror. Nothing.

The clouds frowned. "I can tell you don't recognize me. They would have made sure of that, wouldn't they? I haven't seen you since I held you as a newborn in my arms."

Aurora sucked her teeth. Then she said, "I know *who* you are. *What* are you?"

"I am the Dream King," the cloud rumbled. "I balance the dreamworld and guide the dreams of humanity. I have searched everywhere for you, looking in people's dreams, listening for the signal of your mind. I almost had you several years ago, but your kidnappers hid you again."

"Those weren't my kidnappers! They were Mom and Aunt Matron, the people who love me and cared for me and brought me up..." She broke off.

Mom who'd brought me up...until three years ago when, in terror, she'd hidden me away in some out-of-the-way place and tied me down under layers of false memories that hid who I really was.

She began to understand why she'd felt so angry at her mother, now, and Aunt Matron. *They'd never let me be myself. I wasn't a country waitress trapped in some dead-end village, but I don't know who I am. Mom never told me. Nobody let me find out who I really was.*

Maybe this Dream King could tell me.

But she felt so small under his sky-sized face. *In those eyes, how could I be anything but the smallest insect?*

Keep him talking. Find out what I can but also figure out where I can run if I need to get away from here.

"What do you want?" she shouted.

Laughter rippled across the dead city. Warm, but tinged with—*could that be nerves?*

"You're my daughter, Aurora. I've spent years looking for you. I've abandoned my duties and thought of nothing but you. At last, I've found you, and I can bring you home."

Aurora tried to think of the sort of bedroom she'd have in the Dream King's house. She guessed it wouldn't be the sort of place where you could hang posters.

The cloud face shifted. The eyes widened and the mouth twisted with longing. "Come with me, Aurora. Come home."

Aurora hesitated, staring at the dark clouds. *All the answers are here. I just have to go to him. I just—*

Matron's voice echoed in her head. *It'll be disaster if you do!* The funnel cloud descended. Matron fired her gun.

Aurora took a step back. "No." *I don't want to be a part of something so violent.*

The clouds grew darker. Polk stood at the top of the ladder. "Get ready to run," he hissed.

Polk. He's on my side. He's stayed with me even after I abandoned him. If he's ready to run, so am I.

"Aurora..." The warning thunder rippled across the bricks and asphalt.

"No," she said again. "You didn't ask to see me, you didn't write, you didn't come up to me and introduce yourself. No. You tried to take me by force. You sent a snake man to stalk me! You attacked Matron! You attacked Polk! You attacked me! What father does that to his child?"

Lightning flickered around the edge of the Dream King's face. "They've turned you against me!"

"Listen!" Aurora yelled. "I've lived sixteen years without knowing you. I don't need you in my life, so just send a birthday card next time! Go away!"

Thunder shook the ground. "Come back to me!" The Dream King's face twisted in anger...and kept twisting. The eyes bled black. The cheeks ripped open. The mouth stretched into a gigantic cavern. Darkness spewed out, a thick cloud of black shapes that filled the sky with beating wings. Crows!

Polk darted back and grabbed her arm. "Run! Now!"

The cloud of crows swept closer and closer. Aurora

turned to run. *No,* she thought. *We can't run. We've got to fly!* The words came from some instinct deep inside. *We've got to fly. We can't run; they're too fast. This is a dream, so we've got to make it happen. C'mon, fly! Fly! Make me fly!* In her mind's eye, she imagined a gigantic bird grabbing her up and sweeping her to safety.

She pulled free of Polk's grip and ran toward the parapet. "Polk! Help me! Now!" she shouted, reaching behind her without looking.

A talon gripped her forearm and lifted her off her feet. Aurora looked up in astonishment. A wingspan of a giant kestrel, half the width of the roof, filled her vision. Polk squawked.

"What the hell am I doing?" he screamed. "What's happened to me?" It was Polk's voice, but it came out as a screech from a beak. His talons loosened. Aurora slipped. They sailed over the edge of the building parapet.

She clawed at him, pulling large feathers from his chest. "Hold onto me!" she shouted. "Whatever you do, don't let go!"

"But, how—"

"Shut up and go! Go!"

The cloud of crows was almost upon them. Polk clamped back down on her shoulders. His claws dug in, but Aurora didn't protest. "Faster!" she shouted. She gripped his spindly legs. "Faster!" With a great swoop of his wings, they sailed forward, rising above the buildings.

The crows spread out like buckshot, a cloud that towered over them and stretched across the sky. Polk flapped desperately. The wind beat at Aurora's face and tore at her clothes, but the birds' cries filled her ears. Beneath her, rooftops and squares of green parkland swept past. They followed the sweep of the river that cut through the centre of the city.

"Faster!" she gasped.

Polk squawked. "What's that?"

Aurora looked. A white speck came into view ahead of them. It was a dove, flapping desperately. As it drew closer, they realized, just like Polk, it was huge and flying right at them.

There was no time to avoid it. Aurora yelled and closed her eyes.

The dove shot past, the wind of its wake buffeting Aurora's face. She heard it meet the cloud of crows with a sound like snowballs pelting a brick wall. She grabbed a look over her shoulder and saw the cloud of crows disintegrating. The dove wheeled and clawed, covered in black specks, some of which slipped off and fell to the ground.

But most of the flock swept onward.

Aurora looked around for something she could use to stop them. Flying through the air, there wasn't much at hand. Okay, nothing.

A park stretched out below, along both sides of the river. Behind her, she heard the flapping of wings grow louder. *If only we could hide under the trees,* she thought.

The trees in the park twisted. A webwork of greenery slithered upward, like vines on an invisible trellis. Polk and Aurora shot past it and an impromptu fence of branches rose behind them. The first crows smacked into it and got tangled among the limbs.

Polk flew on.

Gripping his legs, Aurora looked back. The crows buffeted the leafy fence. The sky behind it rumbled and flashed. Then the darkness grew translucent. The plants and the crows faded from sight, and the clouds broke apart and softened into blue. The northern sky was clear again. The giant kestrel and its passenger flew alone over an empty city.

Polk sagged. He grunted with the effort of flapping his wings. They started losing altitude. He gasped. "I...can't..."

Aurora looked ahead to the roof of a high-rise apartment close to them. It also happened to be the tallest building in the city. "There! Set down there."

Polk puffed the distance. Aurora saw the roof rise up faster than she wanted it to and cartwheeled her legs for the landing. As her feet struck gravel, Polk let go, and she sprawled.

He fell forward, his legs giving way as they touched down. He skidded over the roof, turning as he slid from bird to human. He jolted to a stop, then painfully pushed himself up onto human hands and knees. "What...just happened?"

"Sleep," said Aurora. Polk fell forward and lay still, breathing softly. *Like an enchanted prince,* she thought.

Which makes me what? The wicked witch?

But he needs a rest, she told herself firmly. *And I need time to think alone.*

She picked herself up and brushed herself off. She rubbed the spots on her shoulders where Polk's claws had dug in. Then she walked to the roof's edge and leaned against the parapet, staring north at the clear sky. The breeze fluttered in her hair. She thought about what had just happened.

She looked at her hands. She remembered what she'd told Britney.

"You've already imagined a fence, right?" said Aurora, "and it came true?"

Britney nodded. "But he jumped over it," she mumbled.

"And you've already imagined a door, right," Aurora continued. "So you know that you can imagine whatever you want in the dream, and it's right there in front of you. Right?"

And not just the dream, Aurora thought. I asked for a ride, and we found the rail truck. I could stop snakes in mid-strike and make new ones burst from the ground.

And now she was in a dream—in her element, even though she never slept. She could turn Polk into a bird. There was no limit to what she could do.

She looked at her hands again. *No limit at all.*

She walked backwards from the parapet until the whole edge of the roof and the buildings beyond were in view. She closed her eyes. "Let there be a fence," she said.

She opened her eyes. Around her, on the roof inside the parapet, a bare metal fence, a railing with posts, guarded the edge.

She kept her eyes open. "Make it a picket fence!"

The metal turned white. The posts multiplied and aimed points at the sky. The railing became a wooden crosspiece.

She clicked her tongue thoughtfully. She hadn't said what colour. Maybe she'd thought it. "Higher!"

The white pickets stretched up and up, aiming for a vanishing point in the sky.

Lower, she thought.

The pickets shrank down.

Huh, she thought. *I don't even have to talk out loud.*

Stop.

The fence stopped at waist height and stayed like that.

Aurora looked at the high-rise across the street. She motioned at it, palm up.

The building rose like a silent rocket. Floor after floor flicked past her, and then came the foundation, ripped out of the ground, dirt and chunks of concrete streaming off.

She held out her hand, palm down, and lowered her arm. The skyscraper slowed, stopped, then began to descend. It met the ground with a dull thud.

Aurora looked to her left and right, then raised her arms. Every building, every house, every church steeple, every tree, rose slowly into the air. Aurora gently waved her arms, and the waves travelled out across the city, ripples in a sea of cement, steel, masonry and greenery beneath the morning sky.

Aurora dropped her arms to her sides and looked at the undulating skyline. A newfound sense of power rose in her chest and tickled her throat. She laughed.

Okay! Now what?

Polk stirred and muttered in his sleep.

What could I possibly try that would tell me the limits of my power? She looked at the sky. *Okay.* She took a dozen steps backward, focused on the parapet in front of her, and braced herself.

Beside her, Polk rolled over and looked up. "Hey, Aurora. What—?"

Aurora sprinted. The parapet bounced in her field of vision. Beyond it, the Saskatoon cityscape rose into view.

Polk jumped up and ran after her. "Aurora!" He grabbed her just as she cleared the parapet. They fell.

The wind beat at her face. Glass and concrete flashed past. The lines on the road below grew more and more distinct. Behind her, someone was screaming.

As she looked over her shoulder, her arms and legs splayed out like a skydiver, she caught sight of Polk, falling with her, eyes staring and face white against his wind-flattened hair.

Aurora twisted around in mid-air, grabbed his outstretched hand, and pulled him closer. He clutched her desperately. She could just hear his screams over the shriek of the wind in her ears. The ground was getting awfully close.

She closed her eyes and concentrated. She felt the wind ease up. Polk pressed against her as they slowed. She eased herself upright and held onto Polk as they stopped falling. Then she let go of him.

Polk stared at her a long moment, gasping. "What the hell did you do that for?!"

Aurora started to speak, but then she realized that she was out of breath too. She took a moment to catch it. "Just testing a theory."

"What theory?" yelled Polk. "Gravity? News flash, Aurora: it works!"

She grinned. "Not here, it doesn't."

"What—?"

"Two things. One, we just jumped off the tallest building in Saskatoon and didn't get smashed. And two: we didn't actually land."

He looked at his feet. They were standing six feet off the ground. He yelped and fell the rest of the way, landing in a heap.

Aurora giggled.

"That's not funny!" Polk picked himself up off the sidewalk and brushed himself off. He gaped up at her as she floated. He walked around her and underneath her, looking for wires or tricks. Aurora hovered with her hands clasped behind her back.

"What—?"

"This is a dream, remember?" said Aurora.

"Oh." Polk closed his mouth. "So, you thought you'd test it out, and see if you could, what, fly?"

Aurora floated down to the ground. The asphalt scrunched gently underfoot. "Seems to be working."

"That was…" He struggled for the right words. Finally, he said, "That was *insane*! You had no idea if it would work, and you just jumped off a building?"

"Hey, I turned you into a bird, didn't I? Don't you think that's a sign that the normal rules don't apply here?"

"Well, this isn't your personal playground, okay?" Polk stormed off down the road, shaking his head, fists clenched.

"Polk?" Aurora shouted. She ran after him. "Polk, wait!"

He stopped so suddenly that she bumped into him. He

looked around at the buildings floating up and down the
street, rising and falling in their aerial ballet. "Did you do
this?"

Aurora smiled modestly. "Yeah."

"Way not to draw attention to yourself."

She blushed. She swept out her hands, and the buildings sank onto their foundations with the groan of mountains settling.

Polk looked around then strode off towards a high-rise
apartment. Aurora ran to keep up.

The door swung open as they approached. The ground
floor of the building was a mini-mart with aisles of cans
and produce stretched out on either side of the door. Near
the cash, a deli counter offered stools, and seats around
two tables.

"Polk, stop!" Aurora shouted.

"Why don't you just stick a wall in front of me?" he
shouted back. "That'll stop me real quick."

"Polk, I…I won't do that. Please stop?"

He stopped, then turned and looked at her, arms
jammed in pockets, shoulders hunched.

"What's wrong?" Aurora twisted her hands together.
"This is good news, isn't it? We're not as helpless as we
thought."

"You, maybe," said Polk. "Does that give you the right
to turn me into a bird or put me to sleep? Or scare me half
to death with your suicide tricks?"

Or invade your dreams, Aurora thought. She looked at the
floor. "I'm sorry."

He looked at her, then looked away. "It's…okay, I

understand. Well…I don't, but…" He sighed. "I know what it's like. To suddenly discover you have new powers. You want to use them."

She cocked her head. "You have powers too?"

His cheeks flushed. He traced the outline of a tile with his shoe. "Uh…yeah. I haven't told anybody about this. Nobody knows."

"What?"

He looked up at her, then down again. "I can slow down time."

"Slow down time?"

"Yeah."

"Like, can you *stop* time?"

"No."

"Can you speed it up?"

"Er…I never tried. I generally can slow it down just a little, for a little while." He gave her a grin. "I use it to take longer naps."

Aurora covered her mouth. Her shoulders shook.

"It's not funny," he grumbled. "Yeah, I'm a little jealous of you, right now. You have all these powers. My dad seems to have been the king of daydreams or something."

Aurora snorted. She turned away.

"It's not *that* funny!" he snapped. "I mean, it works out well for everybody. I have time to work for Matron, and I get a couple extra hours of sleep."

Aurora burst out laughing. She doubled over. Polk scowled. Then he began to chuckle too. Then they were both laughing, stress and adrenaline pouring out of them.

Aurora drew herself up, wiping the tears from her

cheeks. "I'm sorry." Then, more seriously: "Really, I am. I'm sorry for dragging you into this and for doing all those things to you."

"That's okay, I guess. We were being chased."

"And I'm sorry I looked into your dream and found out how you really felt about me."

His cheeks reddened. "I might have told you, eventually."

She came forward, took a deep breath, and held out her hand. "Friends?"

The flash of disappointment in his eyes lasted only a second. He clasped her hand. "Friends."

He gave a little grunt of surprise as she reached up and clasped the back of his neck, pulled his head down and kissed him. Time slowed as they lingered. Polk put his arms around her and held her tightly. Then she let go and stepped back.

Polk stared at her, his eyes shining.

"Oh, and Polk?"

"Uh-huh?"

She grinned at him. "In your dreams."

He reddened again, but he flashed her a grin. "Careful, there. We're *in* a dream."

She shrugged casually, though her face felt hot. "Yeah? So?"

Suddenly, his grin vanished and he reared back, crying out. His body shook and jerked. Aurora yelled. Polk crashed to the floor, two metal barbs stuck in his back, attached to wires. Salvadore stood over him.

Aurora raised her fists. "You!" she snarled.

He flashed a smile at her and began fishing through his pockets for a new set of wired darts.

"What is this, the *third* time you've tried to grab me?" she said. "I'm surprised the Dream King hasn't fired you."

"Actually," said Salvadore cheerily. "He terminated my employment." He beamed at her. "He didn't like my methods, apparently. Said so after you complained, I was lucky to escape with my life." He found what he was looking for and pulled out a new nozzle for the stun gun. He reloaded. "So that means I'm back to my original plan: to capture you for my own purposes."

"If you hurt me, he'll kill you," she said quietly.

"Actually, I never intended to hand you over to him," said Salvadore. "I was there to thwart his quest. Trust me, I may like my share of screaming, but I'm not stupid. You're a threat to everything, girl. Having something to hold over the Dream King? That's an added bonus. After all, a man in my position has ambitions."

"What do you mean, your position?" said Aurora.

"I'm a number two. An opposing figure, if you will." He shrugged. "Who balances the King of Dreams, girl? Weren't the snakes and spiders enough of a clue?"

Polk struggled up on his hands and knees. Aurora knelt beside him. She looked up at Salvadore. "I get it," she said. "Nightmares."

Salvadore smirked. "I also do bats, standardized tests, and suddenly finding yourself naked with everybody pointing at you and laughing."

Aurora looked past him. A flurry of cans rose up two aisles over, like a metal dust storm. She faced Salvadore.

He slid the new pins into his stun gun and looked up. "So, will you come quietly? Oh, of course not. Silly me." He aimed the device.

There was a sound of clanking feet. It was a strangely heavy, metallic sound, with a hint of sloshing liquid. *Clomp! Clomp! Clomp!*

Crouching on the floor, Polk looked up then scrambled back in horror. Aurora stood up, holding Salvadore's eyes.

Around the end of the aisle, a tall scarecrow figure made of canned vegetables marched into view. It turned and clanked up behind Salvadore. It stopped a pace behind him, bean-can hands on baby-carrot hips.

Salvadore froze. He looked at Aurora, who was smiling.

Tin Can Man reached out and tapped Salvadore gently on the shoulder.

Salvadore turned around. And looked up.

The monster looked down at him and cocked its extra-large can of tomato soup head.

Aurora grinned. "I can do nightmares too."

Salvadore ducked, but not fast enough.

Clonk!

He sailed into the air, cleared the shelves two aisles away and landed in the pineapple display. Tin Can Man clanked slowly after him.

Polk staggered to his feet, clutching his side. Aurora helped him up. "Told you we weren't helpless," she said.

"That..." Polk gasped. "...was evil!"

"No," said Aurora. "*This* is evil." She cackled theatrically and pointed at the ceiling. Her voice echoed from the store's PA system. "Cleanup in aisle three!"

She pulled Polk along two aisles and towards where Salvadore lay in the middle of a mass of rolling pineapples. Polk skidded on a squashed orange. Tin Can Man stood to one side, hands on his hips.

"What are you doing?" asked Polk as Aurora shifted Salvadore to the floor.

"I need to know." She kicked aside a splattered tomato, pushed back a mass of crushed apples and knelt over Salvadore. His head was tilted back and his eyelids fluttered.

"Look at me," she said. *"Look at me."*

He squinted at her blearily.

"What am I?" She stared into his eyes. "Tell me what I am. What we are."

He struggled to look away, but Aurora peered close. Her eyes held him. She could feel the tips of his dreams like invisible tendrils around his head, brushing her face. She reached out with the fingertips of her mind, grabbed one, and pulled.

Salvadore yelled.

Polk started forward, but Aurora put out her hand. She focused on Salvadore again. "Come on," she snarled. "Let me see!"

She pulled harder.

Images burst into her mind.

Matron holds a squalling infant. Dawn lies semi-conscious in her hospital bed.

"What," says Matron slowly, "do we do with the baby?"

Silence rings the room. The other figures stand around, battered. They look at the ceiling or the floor. In a corner, a young Polk sucks his thumb.

"What," says Matron more loudly, "do we do with this baby?"

More silence.

"He won't stop looking for her," says Matron. "I wouldn't if this were my daughter. So we have to hide her. How?"

Salvadore steps forward and brushes fingertips over the newborn's hair. "You know, there is an easier way."

Matron pulls the infant away as Salvadore makes a grab for it. "No, there isn't."

"There is. I can see it's on your mind, Matron. You're saying it to yourself again and again. It would be so much easier, solve so many problems, if this baby were dead."

"That's not who we are," Matron snaps. "That's not what we do!"

"Nonsense!" says Salvadore. "I know what you do to protect the dreams of children, Matron. And as for me, what is fear without the threat of violence? And where is the threat without the act? Death's counterfeit and all that? Shakespeare was more right than he knew."

"No!" Matron shoves him away. Dawn is waking up, her eyelids fluttering.

"What happened?" she mumbles. "Where's my baby? Give me my baby!"

Matron lays Aurora on Dawn's stomach. "Here's your baby," she says softly. She kisses Dawn atop her head. "We'll protect you. But you've got to run."

Aurora blinked back to reality. "What—?"

Salvadore's hand shot up and closed around her throat. She gagged.

"We've never had to deal with someone like you," he

snarled. "We've never had so much power concentrated in two people. He didn't know what to do with it. He doesn't even know what happened! He just exploded because of you. It would be so much easier if you just died, right here, right now."

Aurora gurgled and clawed at the fingers tightening around her neck. Polk shouted, darted forward, skidded on mashed tomatoes, and fell. He slid forward on his hands and feet.

Aurora forced herself to stop trying to claw Salvadore's vice-like hand from her throat and to concentrate on picturing Tin Can Man. She heard it clunk forward, shove Polk out of its way, and then it swung its bean-can hand down hard just as Salvadore looked up. His face went white.

Clonk!

Salvadore's grip relaxed. Aurora pulled free. She stumbled back, gasping, swallowing and massaging her throat. She scowled at Salvadore's slumped form, then looked up at Tin Can Man. The creature raised its arm for another strike.

"Aurora!" Polk shouted.

Aurora raised her hand. Tin Can Man dropped its arm. It tilted its head at her in a questioning way, then fell apart in a clatter of metal and sloshing liquid.

Aurora and Polk staggered to their feet. Polk gave her a look that was edged with something she didn't recognize. Could it have been fear? *No! Why should he be afraid of me?* "C'mon, let's go," she said.

Polk hesitated, looked down at Salvadore, then turned away.

The exit doors swung open for them—they weren't automatic, she noticed; she had just pushed them open with a brief wave of her hand—and they stepped outside.

They stopped in the middle of the empty road and looked around, uncertain.

"What do we do now?" asked Polk.

"The good news is we're not helpless. The bad news is that I don't know what else we can do except run."

"So we run?"

"We can't run forever. That's the even worse news." She took a deep breath. "Well, it'll give us time to think." She thought for a moment. "We head south."

Polk heaved a sigh. "Again? Where now? Regina?"

"We could rest our feet, you know."

Polk's gaze tracked up as she floated five feet into the air above him. She smiled, hands clasped behind her head.

"Show off," he grumbled.

"Try it!" She grinned at him.

"Are you kidding me?'

"Go on, try it!" She waved him up. "It's your dream, too. C'mon, let's have some fun."

Polk looked at his hands and down at his legs. Then he closed his eyes and took a deep breath. He rose slowly into the air.

He opened his eyes again and blinked in astonishment. Then he tried to pick himself up faster. His legs kicked uselessly. All he could do was wait until he was within Aurora's reach. Then she grabbed his hands and pulled him the rest of the way.

Polk looked around at the empty street they hovered

over. He laughed nervously. "'There is no spoon,'" he muttered.

"What?"

"Never mind."

She let go of his hands and floated back a few paces. "Shall we fly? Easier than walking."

"Fly? Like..." He smiled and threw out his arms. As he moved, he changed. White feathers sprouted all over him. A gigantic kestrel flapped in the air. Off he flew.

Aurora laughed. "Oh, no, you don't! You're not beating me in this race!"

She threw out her arms, changing her own shape. Feathers caught the air and brushed the high-rise windows as she swept forward after him. The floors of each building became a blur as she flew after Polk.

They banked and cartwheeled, dodging between the buildings, Aurora chasing Polk. Their squawking laughter echoed off the glassy towers. Then, looking back at her, Polk let out a squawk of fear. He flew to a parapet and perched, staring down at her. Aurora flapped up beside him. He scuttled back a few steps.

"What?" She looked at him with first her right eye and then her left.

His head bobbed nervously. "N... nothing. It's all good."

She opened her beak to call him a liar. Then she saw her reflection in the glassy side of a tower across the street.

The reflection of a giant crow stared back at her.

CHAPTER NINE:
AURORA ASCENDS

AURORA STOOD WITH HER HANDS IN HER JACKET pockets. She turned slowly, keeping Roger in view as he circled.

"I didn't think you'd come," he said.

"Here I am."

His fists were clenched and his shoulders tense, but she could see the confusion in his eyes. She heard the slight quiver in his voice.

Nobody's ever pushed him like this before, she thought. He isn't sure what to do next.

"I'm not afraid of you," she said.

"You're in for a world of hurt," he snarled.

That sounds just like the TV shows he loves. I can just see him watching cop shows and cheering on the criminals.

A part of him wants to back down, but he won't. He is bigger than me, and he knows how to hit things. He could hurt me, if I let him. But I'm not going to let him.

I'm going to change the rules.

"You be careful," she said.

"Think you can beat me?" He laughed loudly.

"Maybe."

"Well?" he demanded.

"Well what?"

"Are you going to put 'em up, or what?"

Aurora tilted her head. "Why?"

"To fight, of course. Or are you scared?"

Here goes nothing. Her grin showed her teeth. "I'm not scared. But you should be."

Roger laughed, but now he sounded unsure.

"He's coming for you, Roger," said Aurora.

He shook his head. "What are you talking—?"

"Remember the contract?"

He froze. Aurora pressed on. "You signed it. You signed it in *blood*. There's no getting out now that he's coming for you."

"What are you talking about?" The colour had drained from his face.

"What did you sell your soul for, Roger?" Aurora began to circle him. "So you could hit people?"

"It was just a dream!" He took a step back, tripped and fell. Gasps came all around. He scrambled up. "I saw it in a movie. It's not real. It was just a dream."

Aurora chuckled. "If it was just a dream, Roger, how would I know?" She leaned towards him. "Can't you hear it? Can't you feel it?"

Sweat ran down his face. And to her surprise, Aurora heard a distant rumble. She felt the ground shake. It was already dark, thanks to the socks over the lamps, but now the light was going out of the sky. She could feel heat rising from behind Roger's back.

The other kids crowded forward, whispering at each

other, with no idea what was going on. This was all happening in Roger's head. She was making the dream play out for real in front of his eyes. And she was inside his dream. She could see what he saw.

She grinned. *I can use this.*

She threw her arms wide. "He's here!"

Flames leaped up in Roger's vision. The ground cracked and smoked. Aurora cackled. Roger yelled.

In her vision, the buildings became the walls of Roger's bedroom, draped in shadow and fear. A mailbox became a distorted version of his chest of drawers. A doorway was his closet door. It shuddered under the pounding of something inside. Roger crouched in his bed, knees to his chest, shaking. She could see Roger's vision of Albijana superimposed on reality. As the girl stared in the real world, perplexed, Roger saw wings of smoke and ash brush against his bedroom wall and flash with flame. Albijana opened her mouth, and he saw a mouth of fangs surrounding a cavern of fire.

Roger curled up into a ball on the concrete. He sobbed hysterically. "Mommy! Mommy! Make it stop! Make it go away! Make me wake up! Mommy!" His cries filled the alleyway.

The kids crowded around, eyes wide. "What's wrong with him?" The crowd jostled, and Anne burst through, dragging Mr. Singh, the owner of the corner store, behind her.

Albijana was at Aurora's side but not too near. "What did you do? What did you do?!"

"What d'you think? I fixed him. I paid him back."

Aurora turned back to Roger. Her triumphant grin
faded. Mr. Singh was kneeling beside him, trying to touch
him as Roger flinched. Finally, Mr. Singh picked up Roger
while the boy screamed.

The crowd melted away. Albijana went with them.
Aurora watched them go. Twilight deepened to night.

Aurora stood alone. *What have I done?*

"It was just his dream," she muttered. "He'll be okay."

She shoved her hands in her jacket pockets and started
home. A squawk made her stop and turn around.

In the light of a streetlamp, Aurora saw a crow perched
on a branch. It looked at her with one eye and then the
other. It cawed once. Then it stretched out its wings and
flew away.

Now Aurora stared at her distant reflection in horror for
a long moment. Polk stepped back from the roof edge,
changing back into a teenaged boy.

Aurora changed back too. She kept staring at her reflection across the street. Her breath shook. "I'm a crow!"

Polk took a step away.

"I didn't tell myself to become a crow," she went on.
"I just said bird, and the dreamscape changed me into the
most natural form it could find. So, I'm a crow."

"Aurora..."

"The Dream King only sends out crows."

"Aurora, don't worry about this." Polk's voice was desperately calm.

"It really is true. I really am his daughter. No wonder

he's been looking for me after all this time. He'll never stop unless I find him first."

Polk shifted on his feet. Something about the noise made her turn around. Polk had pulled a dagger from his sleeve. The light glittered off the tarnished bronze and played over runes that decorated its hilt.

She raised her eyebrows. "Is that for me?" she asked quietly.

Polk's Adam's apple bobbed. "Yes." His knuckles were white on the hilt. His face was as white as his knuckles.

"You said you swore to protect me."

"And to—" He swallowed. "To kill you if you ever turned toward the Dream King." The blade started to shake.

"Polk," said Aurora levelly. "I'm stronger than you."

"Yes."

"We're in the dream world, and I can move buildings with the power of my mind."

He nodded slowly. "Yes."

"I could crush you like a bug."

"Yes."

"And *you* are going to kill *me*?"

He grimaced. "That's what I swore."

"Okay." She tilted her head. "Do it."

He drew back sharply.

Aurora clasped her hands behind her back. "You have your orders, Polk. I won't stop you. Do it."

He looked from her to his knife and back again. He raised the knife high. He let out a yell. The blade swept down. Aurora closed her eyes.

She waited.

She opened her eyes. The point of the knife had stopped inches from her chest. Polk's hands trembled. Tears trickled down his cheeks.

She stared at the knifepoint hovering in front of her a long moment. She hadn't stopped it. Polk had. The knife fell to the ground with a clatter. He sobbed. "I can't."

She put her arms around him. He embraced her. She pulled his face to hers and their lips met. They held the kiss a long moment, savouring the pressure of their lips and the taste of each other's tongues. When he let go, he cradled his head on her shoulder.

"Don't go," he whispered in her ear. "For God's sake, please don't go to him."

She straightened up, looked him in the eye. "I have to. I'm sorry."

His hands tightened on his shoulders. "No!"

She turned into a giant crow and beat him back with her wings.

☙

Polk snapped awake. He staggered back against the hood of a car, stunned by the sudden uproar of traffic. He gasped in the heat radiating off the asphalt of the parking lot. The bowling alley where they'd flown from the Dream King stood just behind him.

He looked around. Aurora wasn't there.

But a woman was striding towards him, a baseball bat in her hand.

"Dr. Perrault? What are you do—?"

The air left him as Dawn swung the bat into his stomach.

"I know what your orders were, Polk." She pulled back on the bat. "I know what you swore to do, and I'm *not* letting you get anywhere near Aurora."

Polk straightened up, wheezing. "No…wait…I'm not—" He grunted as she hit him again, in the chest. "Please! Let me explain!"

"You stay away from my daughter!" She yelled and swung the bat. She caught him hard between the legs.

⚜

Aurora stood on the roof of the tallest building in Saskatoon. She looked around once, then ran to the parapet, hopping onto it, her sneakers turning to claws and her arms to wings and her clothes to feathers. As a gigantic crow, she looked down on the trees, the buildings and the grid-like streets.

I'm ready.

Where would the Dream King's headquarters be? If he's in the realm of dreams, then he could be anywhere: a mystical portal in the middle of a farmer's field or a deep pit at the bottom of the sea. Perhaps I only have to choose the location, and it would be there.

Down below, she could see the people: ghostly images, shadows in overcoats, walking with hunched shoulders, as if in rain. She couldn't see their faces.

But hadn't the Dream King pulled all the people out of the dreamworld? Maybe he'd just pulled them out of this dream? But people never stop dreaming, even when they're awake. Where do they go? As she looked down at the ghostly forms slipping through the streets, she wondered, *am I looking down at all the dreams?*

If bad things happen when I meet the Dream King, then let's meet far, far away from here; a place far from everyone.

She scanned the skies and saw a star, twinkling, bright even in the rising daylight.

There, she thought. *Meet me there.*

Aurora spread her wings and launched into the sky.

The air cooled rapidly. She shot through clouds, sudden blinding whiteness, then out into seas of cobalt blue. The air thinned. She beat up and up until the sky filled with stars in broad daylight and she could see the curve of the earth. Then she spread her wings and ran her gaze along the horizon. Far below, Saskatchewan was a patchwork quilt dotted with bursts of cotton batting.

Where was it? C'mon, she thought. *Show yourself!*

She felt her gaze turn as if it was hooked, to look at the eastern horizon. A star on the edge of space twinkled.

She angled her wings and shot forward at the speed of dreams. The twinkle grew brighter.

As she flew, she heard distant ripples of sound. People shouting "Aurora!" Her mother's voice. "Aurora!" Polk's. She ignored them.

The twinkle faded, but, finally, she was there. Hovering in mid-air, she stared at the shape in front of her.

It was a door. A simple wood-panel door, unpainted, with a brass doorknob on a concrete step with a "Welcome" mat in front of it, where sky met space. Aurora tilted her head one way, then the other, waiting for it to change, to open, but it just sat there, waiting for her hand.

She flapped closer, talon reaching for the doorknob.

A gigantic dove shot up from below and struck her full in the chest.

Aurora cartwheeled, screeching in pain and anger. White feathers beat at her, filling her vision. She struck back with her black wings. The dove fell back.

She looked around. Distant specks, white, black and grey, were rising into the sky. There were dozens—no, hundreds—and they were flying right at her.

She squawked angrily. *You think you're going to stop me?* She turned back to the door, but the gigantic dove swept on her again, its claws gouging at her wings. Aurora screamed. "Leave me alone!"

She twisted and pecked hard at the dove's chest. It crumpled but held on to her. They fell, spinning, like a broken plane out of the sky.

Aurora held the big dove tight in her claws and gazed deep into its beady black eyes. "Who are you, and why are you doing this?" she screeched.

The dream hit her like a grenade exploding.

Matron bursts from the elevator into the Maternity reception area. A dozen eyes stare at her from the waiting room. A boy, barely a toddler, sucks his thumb.

Matron blanches. "Polk?" She rounds on his father. "What's he doing here? What are you all doing here?"

"Your brother invited us," says Polk's father.

The head nurse steps behind Matron and clears her throat. "Can I help you?"

Matron whirls around. "Where is Dawn Perrault?"

"Who are you?"

"Don't waste time, woman," Matron shouts. "Where is she?"

Salvadore stands up from his seat in the waiting room, his eyes sparkling with mischief. "Matron? What's wrong?"

The head nurse bristles. "Dawn Perrault is currently in a birthing room. The labour is going well. The father of the baby is with her. Are you related to the family?"

"Idiot." Matron pushes past the nurse. "Get him out of there!"

The nurse grabs Matron. "If you're not directly related to the mother, I can't let you go into the birthing room. Madam, if you continue, I'll have to call security!"

"I'm his sister!" Matron shouts. "He doesn't know what he's dealing with!"

A cry makes both women stop. A baby squawks.

"There, now," says a midwife in a nearby room. "There—"

The midwife screams.

Then a doctor.

Then the nurses in the next room over.

People rush for the emergency exit, pushing past the people in the waiting room who have stood up one after the other.

The head nurse rushes forward. "What's happening?" She runs partway down the corridor, then stops. She looks at her hands, eyes widening. She flexes her fingers and screams.

Matron shoves her toward the emergency exit. "Go! Get out while you still can!"

The hospital corridor twists, oozing like lava. Shadows

Aurora broke out of the dream. She was still falling, still clawing the giant dove. The ground loomed closer.

"Matron?" She'd meant to say it, but the words came from everywhere.

"You have to stop!" Matron's claws dug in.

"No!"

"Stop, girl, or else—"

"Or else what?" Aurora snarled back. "You'll kill me?"

"If I have to!"

"Go ahead and try!" Aurora stabbed wildly. Her beak sunk deep into Matron's shoulder. Red spilled across the dove's white chest and flecked Aurora's face. The dove screamed. The claws loosened, and Aurora pulled free. She soared.

"Aurora!" Matron screamed, struggling to stay aloft with one broken wing. Aurora watched as Matron lost altitude. A lump formed in her throat. Down Matron fell, until she became a speck against the ground. Then her wings swept wide, and she sailed across the patchwork quilt. Aurora let out the breath she was holding.

She looked around her. The air was becoming full of sounds: bird cries, bat screeches, snake hisses, the chitter of insects. She'd forgotten about the oncoming flying things. They were closing in on her.

Aurora turned towards the door. It had changed back to a sparkle of light. She angled up, and a gigantic bat swept forward and caught her full on the chest.

The air left her. Her body changed. She was Aurora, a teenaged girl now, though her arms were still crow's wings.

She beat the bat off and sent it flying with a kick. She beat her wings and sailed up towards the sparkle of light.

The creatures were like a cloud, now, wings and arms and talons clawing at her feet as she struggled for every last beat of air. Their cries buffeted her ears. Something grabbed her sneakers. She let her shoes slip off and soared up barefoot.

She landed on the concrete doorstep, wings changing to arms. She grabbed the doorknob. The door opened inward. Darkness yawned.

Something grabbed her ankle, and Aurora fell against the doorstep. She lay, limbs splayed, for a moment transfixed by a face of statuesque light, like an angel. Its beautiful mouth opened into a gaping hole lined with fangs. Its wings snapped like sails.

She threw the welcome mat at it, then kicked it in the face. It let go. More arms grabbed at her over the doorstep. Aurora crabwalked backward into the darkness.

The door slammed, and darkness took her.

CHAPTER TEN:
HER TERRIBLE SLEEPING BEAUTY

AURORA LAY A LONG MOMENT IN BLIND SILENCE, not even sure if she had a body.

Gradually, she became aware of her heart racing. She lay a moment longer, breathing slowly while the beats slowed down. She sat up. "Where am I?"

She reached out and found walls on either side of her. Keeping a hand on one wall, she walked forward for several minutes, aware only of the echo of her feet and the smoothness of the walls. A spark of light appeared ahead and gradually turned into a square. Aurora dropped her caution and rushed towards it.

Stepping out into the light, she stopped and looked down at herself. Her clothes had changed. In place of her jeans and T-shirt, she wore a long, black cloak over a shimmering, black, sleeveless, ankle-length dress. The black shoes on her feet had heels.

She stood in the doorway of a gigantic ballroom. It was bigger than a football field. Translucent columns held up a vaulted ceiling of stars. A black and white marble floor stretched in all directions.

Aurora stepped into the ballroom. Her footfalls echoed.

She walked and walked. She seemed to walk miles before reaching the middle of the gigantic room. She stopped there and turned in a slow circle. Nobody else was here.

Then a piano started playing. Aurora whirled around but saw nothing. The music continued, tinny, like the sound of the old upright her ballet teacher had used during dance class, rattling off a rapid waltz.

One-two-three, one-two-three...

As Aurora turned, her feet took up the rhythm. She stopped them and stood still, but it was hard to resist the urge to tap.

One-two-three, one-two-three...

More instruments joined the waltz: a pipe organ and drums that resonated in the chest. An unseen woman belted out lyrics. Aurora almost recognized the song.

Around her, figures rose up through the floor like ghosts, their limbs jerking robot-like in time with the music. In moments the hall was filled with dancers. They all wore fancy dress, modern, Victorian and Renaissance. Their faces were as blank as mannequins.

Someone tapped on her shoulder. Aurora turned with a start. The nearest figure bowed low and extended his hand to her.

"I don't—" Aurora began, but the man took her hand, put his other hand on her side, and turned her into the dance. To her surprise, she followed his steps with ease, heels, dress and all.

The other dancers paired off and began to circle in time with the music, tracing intricate patterns across the floor.

One-two-three, one-two-three...

Aurora's mannequin partner turned her. She twirled and found another hand reaching for hers. In time with the music, she took it, twirled again, and found herself in the arms of Salvadore, who wore an evening suit with a plum-coloured brocade vest.

He leered at her. "You dance divinely, my dear."

"Trust me, it's not by choice," Aurora growled. The waltz rhythm made her words come out staccato-style.

"Not by my choice either, I fear," said Salvadore. "But since I'm trapped in this dance, I might as well enjoy the company."

He twirled her around. Aurora spun on the balls of her feet but couldn't let go of the tips of his fingers before she came twisting back. He caught her in a graceful dip.

One-two-three, one-two-three...

He pulled her up. Aurora felt breathless. "If you're trapped here, who's trapping you? Who are all these... things?" She tipped her head at the mannequins.

"*You've* trapped me here, darling girl," said Salvadore. "You and your father. This—" He grunted in frustration as the music twirled her away again. Aurora found herself reaching for another hand, twirling into another man's arms. She blinked up at his face.

"This is your dream," said Polk, looking unnaturally grand in his tuxedo and bow tie. "Yours and the Dream King's. The others can't be more than ghosts to you, here. Salvadore and me...we're the only ones strong enough to break through to talk to you."

He pulled her into a dip. Aurora arched her back then came up suddenly, her hands clasping the back of his neck.

"How did you get here?" she asked.

"I had help."

She tilted her head to get a good look at him. "And how did you get that black eye?"

He grinned ruefully. "Again...I had help."

They switched partners again. Aurora blinked at the new face. "Mom?! You have special powers too?"

"Of course!" Her mother wore a low-cut, ankle-length red dress. "I'm a certified psychologist."

One-two-three, one-two-three...

"Aurora," said her mother, as they did a back-to-back turn. "You've got to get away from here before the Dream King finds you."

"Is he here?" Aurora looked around. They switched partners again.

"He's over there." Salvadore nodded toward a table at the head of the room. Aurora hadn't noticed it before, but a shadowy figure loomed there. "He's coming for you," Salvadore said.

"Good," said Aurora. "Let's finish this."

She tried to twirl out of Salvadore's hold, but the beat and his sudden tug pulled her back.

"Listen to me, you foolish girl!" he hissed. "I may like to cause a little chaos, spread a little fear, but there are limits. I pretended to help the Dream King so I could hamper his search. You have to stay away from him!"

"But why? Why?"

They swapped partners again, and Aurora found herself staring into her mother's face.

"Everyone has been telling you to stay away from him!

Even Salvadore, the Nightmare King. Maybe you should listen?"

"But Mom! He's my father. He won't stop coming for me, and I can't stop him. I'm not going to live the rest of my life on the run. This has to end, one way or another."

"I would rather die than have anything happen to you. But it's not just you."

"What are you talking about?" Aurora's voice rose. "Why did you run away from him? What happened?"

Her mother started to say something, but the music switched partners again, and Aurora was face-to-face with Polk. Beyond him, she could see that the Dream King had moved away from the table at the end of the room and was standing at the edge of the dance floor.

One-two-three, one-two-three...

"I told you the Dream King killed my parents," said Polk. "I don't think he meant to, but he did, the moment you were born."

"How?"

"I don't know. I was there, but I was too young, and it was all so confusing. I don't really remember. But it was bad." He looked over Aurora's shoulder and his face tightened. She looked back to see the dark figure moving through the dancing crowd toward her.

"Aurora, please, *please* get out of here!"

"Not until someone tells me what happened!"

They switched partners again, and now she was with her mother.

"I was almost out of it from the labour," said her mom. "Then dreams started breaking into the real world. Monsters. Stuff out of nightmares. At first, I thought it was the drugs they used on me, but it wasn't."

Aurora frowned. "Why would nightmares break out into the real world?"

Dawn shook her head. "I don't know. Nobody knows. Matron once said that maybe they were afraid of what awaited them in the dreamworld."

"*He* did that?" Aurora looked back through the crowd. "Why would he do that?"

"I don't know. But it got a lot worse until his people came and separated us. They told me to hide myself and you. And I did. I was terrified. I ran from my practice in Toronto to a school counsellor's job in Winnipeg. But it wasn't far enough."

She looked over Aurora's shoulder, and her breath caught. "Aurora, he's right behind you. Run!"

"I can't!"

They switched partners again. The Dream King reached for Aurora. Aurora reached out to take his hand. Before she could, Dawn cut in. Aurora tried to grab her mother, but Polk snatched Aurora's hand and danced away. Aurora strained to look over her shoulder.

One-two-three, one-two-three...

"Hi," said Dawn with a squeak. "Fancy meeting you here!"

The Dream King smiled. "Dawn. It's been sixteen years," the Dream King rumbled. "In your time."

"That long?" Dawn said sarcastically.

"You're distracting me."

"Glad I can still do that."

One-two-three, one-two-three...

His expression softened. As they twirled past Aurora, he played with a strand of Dawn's hair. "Dawn, the Dreamwalker with the golden hair."

"It's going silver."

"Gold, silver, it's still precious." His face darkened. "Why did you leave me?"

"Don't you remember?"

Shadows clouded his eyes. "I can only remember reaching out to hold our child. Then I blacked out. After I woke up, nobody would let me see you or her."

"I'm sorry. I…I missed you."

Aurora struggled to pull her hands from Polk's grip. "Polk! Let me go!" But the music bound her to him.

"We've got to get away," said Polk. "Just listen to me, please. We can dance to the side of the—"

He let out a yowl when she head-butted his nose.

"I've spent sixteen years searching for you," the Dream King said to Dawn. "I almost found you three years ago, but you disappeared on me again. Let me see our daughter."

Tears ran down her cheeks. "I can't."

"Dawn," the Dream King rumbled. "Don't try to stop me."

"Please," Dawn began. "Don't—"

"Enough!" He flung his arms wide. There was a rush of air. The walls and ceiling disappeared. The music stopped. The dancers vanished. Across a marble checkerboard dance floor stretched out beneath a dome of stars, five people stood: the Dream King and Aurora facing each other, with Polk, Dawn and Salvadore between them.

There was a long moment of silence. Everyone looked from one to the other. The Dream King held out his hands. "Now. Aurora, come to me."

Aurora brushed down her dress. She took a step, then choked as Salvadore's arm went around her neck. Dawn, Polk and the Dream King started forward, then froze. Salvadore held an obsidian blade to Aurora's throat.

"I'm sorry, everyone," Salvadore said, smiling as Aurora gagged. "It's the only way out. Aurora should have died sixteen years ago, and she would have, if Matron hadn't gotten in the way."

He grunted as Aurora jabbed his stomach with her elbow. She twisted out of his arms and kicked him hard in the gut, doubling him over. Then she drew a line in the air in front of her with her finger. There was a rush of wind. From beyond one side of the checkerboard, a church steeple rose into view, cutting through the wall-less ballroom like a knife through butter.

Salvadore's mouth opened as the stonework as it whipped towards him. The steeple caught him, and carried him to the other side, where he vanished.

Polk winced. "Ow."

Dawn stared at her daughter, her hand over her mouth.

Aurora turned. She looked across the dance floor, past Polk and Dawn. The Dream King met her eyes. "Aurora."

"Dad...?"

"You came."

"I had no choice." Aurora took a shaky breath. "I realized I was my father's daughter."

"Why didn't you come when I told you?"

"I didn't...want to believe it. But I do now."

He opened his arms. "Come here, Aurora."

"Stop!" Polk planted himself between them. "Just...stop for a minute. Think about what you're doing! Think about what's happening! Didn't either of you watch Salvadore when Aurora hit him? He smiled! Aurora hit him with a church, and he looked *relieved*! Who'd rather be hit by a church than spend another minute here?"

Aurora frowned. The Dream King fumed. "Stand aside. No one takes my daughter away from me."

Dawn caught the Dream King's arm. "Please. Let's just talk about this. I don't know what happened when Aurora was born." She glanced at the ballroom around her, looking overwhelmed. "I don't even know how you could possibly have been interested in me."

The Dream King smiled at her. "I fell in love with you, Dawn."

"How?" said Dawn, her voice small. "Why?"

"You called her a Dreamwalker," said Polk. "Why?"

"She's a human who can lend her power to others so they can control their dreams," said the Dream King. He touched her hair. "Most humans shield themselves from the dream world. They wake up. They say, 'It's only a dream'. Very few ride the currents and take control."

Dawn frowned. "But that doesn't make sense. I'm just a psychologist—a hypnotherapist."

"You are more than that," said the Dream King. "You entranced me as soon as I saw you guide the dreams of that little girl. In another time and place, you'd be a priestess."

"Or a witch," Polk muttered. "A human who can help others control their dreams. Put that together with the Dream King. What would their child be like?"

Aurora looked at him sharply.

"Enough," the Dream King snapped, "Aurora, I'm sorry. I wish I had been there to see you grow up. Would you come to me, now?" He hesitated, then added, "Please?"

Aurora stepped back. She looked from Dawn to Polk and then to the Dream King and back. The moment stretched. Then she strode forward. The Dream King stepped forward to meet her. Polk stepped in front of Aurora; Dawn stood in front of the Dream King. Aurora pushed Polk aside, while the Dream King picked up Dawn and planted her behind him. Then father and daughter met in the middle of the dance floor and embraced.

"I missed you," she whispered into his shoulder. It was a stupid thing to say, but it felt true. She missed something she had never had.

"Stop!" Polk shouted. "You're going to destroy the world!"

Aurora turned, letting out a laugh of shock and disbelief.

Polk drove on. "Nobody knows what really happened sixteen years ago," he said. "But I think I can guess now. Salvadore said the Dream King exploded. We ride around in dreams. We have access to forces humans can only dream about. But Dawn *controls* those forces; that's what humans do! Something happened when you held Aurora." He waved his arms, desperate. "Like something being put together! Like something reaching critical mass!"

The Dream King's gaze clouded. "I did nothing wrong!"

"Maybe you didn't intend to," said Polk, "but you said Dawn can enter people's dreams and tame them. What if that ability passed to her daughter? When Aurora was placed in the arms of the one being who had the greatest access to the Dreamworld, you had the tool to control the Dreamworld lying in your arms."

The Dream King shook his head. "You don't know what you're talking about."

"You can do everything in your dreams. Put that power over the Dreamworld together, and you have a god," said Polk, "and only a god could use that power the right way. If anybody else gets that kind of power, it would turn them into a…a monster."

The Dream King started towards Polk. Aurora held him back.

"You are not a god," Polk went on. "But you drained Aurora! You took her power into you without even thinking. And all of a sudden, you had the powers of a god. You couldn't control yourself."

The Dream King pinched the bridge of his nose. "Shut up."

"You killed a lot of people," Polk went on. "No wonder you don't remember what happened!"

"Shut up!" The Dream King's voice shook. "How *dare* you suggest I'd harm my daughter?" He coughed, then took a wheezing breath. "After all I've sacrificed in finding Aurora, how can you think that I would ever consider draining her life from her—?"

"You're draining her *right now!*" Polk shouted. "I can see it in the air between you two! Look!"

Dawn and the Dream King looked. The Dream King shook his head blearily. Dawn gasped. A column of haze rippled out from the Dream King, surrounding Aurora. Aurora tried to swipe the cloud away, but it clung to her.

Polk made a sound like he'd been punched. "No...you're not drawing power from her, she's—"

The palms of Aurora's hands glowed. She stared at them.

The Dream King fell to his knees.

Aurora staggered as the glow spread over her whole body. "What's happening?"

Polk and Dawn ran to her. Dawn arrived first, catching Aurora as she fell. Then she cried out and dropped her daughter, staring at her singed hands. Polk skidded to a halt and stared at Aurora's prone form, open-mouthed.

"Polk? Mom?" Aurora gasped. "I feel...strange..."

"Aurora!" Polk shouted into her ear. "Come on! We've got to get you out of here!"

The Dream King fell forward and lay still.

Aurora sat up and pushed Polk away. "But...I can...see." She fumbled around blindly. Her irises had disappeared into black pools. "Mom, the whole world is dreaming inside my head. I can see...everything."

She shuddered. "And they're afraid."

Dawn knelt close. "Aurora, don't go there. You'll be swamped!"

"She's right," said Polk. "Aurora, stop! You can't control the power!" He grabbed her shoulders. His palms smoked.

Aurora's voice dropped an octave. "I don't want to stop. Go away!"

She tossed him off the ballroom floor and into space.

Dawn ran to the edge of the floor and found Polk clinging for dear life, his legs dangling over clouds. She grabbed his arm. Her feet skidded on the marble tiles as she struggled to pull him up onto the dance floor. He looked across the remains of the ballroom at Aurora.

Aurora stood up with the grace of a dancer. The air twisted around her and gave her wings of shadow. Night ran through her veins. Night coloured her lips. Night blotted out her blonde hair.

"I am so big," she whispered, though her voice echoed across the world. "I am so very big, and everyone else is so small, so afraid of the nightmares. They are surrounded by monsters, real and dream. Why doesn't anybody do anything about it?"

She closed her eyes. When she opened them again, the whites of her eyes were black.

"I'm going to do something about it."

"No!" Polk yelled.

Aurora threw back her head and arms. Her spine arched. Her mouth gaped open, and she breathed out a cloud of crows.

They spewed out and up into the sky, spiralling in every direction, line after line of them, a black hurricane gushing from the mouth of the glowing girl. Hundreds. Thousands. Tens of thousands. Millions. Eight billion.

Polk and Dawn cowered as the sky went black.

In her home, Britney walks up the stairs to her bedroom when she stops in her tracks. Her eyes go wide. "No!" she yells. "No! Poor Mr. Scaly! No!" She screams. Her parents can't calm her down.

♩

Aurora felt as though she were being swept along a river of herself, drowning in her power, in her anger, in her sense of other people's fears.

I can use this, she thought. *I can use this. Use it!*

Power coursed through her and lanced all parts of the world. Monsters, dream and human, collapsed and died. Aurora felt the world's fear turn. She heard the screams intensify. In her mind's eye, she saw Britney look up, cowering, beside the remains of Mr. Scaly.

They were still afraid. But now they were afraid of *her*.

Good. They should be. I can use this.

Then a small part of her mind spoke up: *Wait. This isn't me. I don't want to be feared!* She tried to turn against the power, but it was like swimming up a waterfall. It swamped her, smothered her.

What are you doing? asked the voice of her power, her voice. *How can you turn this away? It's yours: take it! Be who you were born to be! Let the world cower at your feet!*

No, she thought. *This isn't me.*

Then what are you? A waitress? A fugitive? A little girl swept from one hidey-hole to another by her terrified mother? Some small thing?

No, she thought. *That isn't me, either.*

She redoubled her efforts to break free, but it was no use. She was a cork in the torrent. As she swept downstream, she scrambled for a rope, an anchor, anything.

Her mind reached out. *Polk!*

🪶

Polk and Dawn scrabbled for purchase against the edge of the dance floor. Beyond and below, the clouds loomed.

Then a flutter of wings brushed near them, and talons settled beside them, transforming into sensible shoes. Matron knelt and gripped Polk's wrist. "Hold on!" She helped Dawn haul him to his feet.

"Matron!" Polk cried over the deafening scream of crows. "Thank God you're here."

Matron shook her head. She rubbed her shoulder. "I'm too late." She looked grimly at Aurora's slumped form and the hurricane of darkness gushing out of her. "I'm way too late."

"What's happening?" Dawn shouted.

"The world is meeting its Dream Queen. They're screaming in terror."

"We have to do something!" Dawn yelled. "Wake her

up, somehow—" She started forward, but Matron pulled her back.

"You touch her, now, you'll be incinerated. How do you stop the wrath of a god?"

Aurora's voice echoed in their heads. *Polk!*

Matron flinched and covered her ears.

Polk, help me!

Matron looked up. "I don't believe it. There's still a part of her alive in there. I didn't think anything could hold out against that power."

Polk! Aurora's voice wavered. *Polk, please? Can you hear me?*

Matron pulled Polk forward. "Answer her! She can hear you. She can hear everything."

Polk called into the air. "Aurora?"

I need...an anchor. Something. The power is blowing me all over the place. I can't hold on!

Polk frowned. "I don't understand!"

Break the connection!

"What?"

Wake me up!

"How?" Dawn pinched her wrists red. "We can't even wake ourselves up."

"I know a way," said Matron. She looked Polk in the eye. "Polk, I can wake you up. When I do, you find Aurora and wake her up. She'll be close. Will you do it?"

"Why can't *you* wake her up?" he asked.

"It's not that easy," Matron shouted over the uproar of the crows. "We're stuck in the Dream King's dream. I can't get out. And even if I could, it wouldn't matter."

"Why not?"

"She asked for you!" Matron yelled. "Will you help her?"

"Of course I will!" shouted Polk.

"You're sure now?" Matron gripped his arm, hard. "Are you really sure? You want to be her Prince Charming? Because it won't be pleasant, and it comes with a cost."

"I'm sure!" Polk yelled. "I love her! I'll do anything for her! Anything!"

Matron sniffed. "Good boy."

Then she threw him into space.

❧

Polk fell, screaming.

He could feel the air escaping his lungs, but all he heard was the rush of wind in his ears.

They say you're dead before you hit the ground, don't they? A part of him hoped so. But they also said that if you died in your dreams, you died in real life. He didn't want to die. His mind and heart raced.

I've been a bird twice. I could fly. Fly! He threw out his arms.

No. Matron's voice whispered in his ears. No feathers appeared.

"Matron? What the hell are you doing?"

He burst out of a cloud. The patchwork quilt of Saskatchewan spread out before him. *Crap! This is going to hurt!*

Maybe I don't need feathers. Aurora hadn't. She'd thrown herself off a building and stopped before hitting the ground. If she could do it, I can do it. I could float. Float!

Do you want to help her or not? said Matron.

"Matron?!" Polk sobbed as the wind whipped past him. "For the love of—"

I'm sorry, son.

The details of the ground grew alarmingly distinct.

There must be a way out of this! There must!

He thought about slowing down time, but what good would that do? It would only prolong the agony.

Wake up! Wake up!! Wake up!!!

His eyes tracked down to the rapidly rising ground, and he closed them. Then he opened them and looked again. He was directly over a farmer's field. There were hay bales everywhere, and he was falling straight for the largest.

His heart lifted. *Maybe I'm going to make it! Maybe...*

Then he looked closer at the hay bale, and the colour drained from his cheeks.

Poking out from the hay bales were pitchforks.

Polk woke screaming.

He lay a moment, gasping, then patted his chest and arms, checking for holes, before slumping on the gravel, breathing heavily. His mind cartwheeled with relief. *It had all been a dream. It had all been just a—*

Wait a minute.

As Polk realized that the fact it was all a dream shouldn't be a relief, another part of his mind asked: *What am I doing on a roof?*

He sat up, then stood up, staggering. Ignoring the ringing in his ears, and a headache that pressed against an eye, he looked around. He stood on the roof of the 5-Pin Bowl-erama. He jumped to see Aurora lying on the gravel next to him, her eyes closed. Her body jerked as if in seizure.

Around him, Saskatoon roared.

Sirens bellowed across the city. Screams echoed off the buildings. In the street below, firefighters at the scene of an accident were spraying the fire hose at unseen monsters. Above him, a plane passed so low, he ducked and gagged in the exhaust of its engines.

He shook his head to clear it. "Wake her up. Right. Let's get on it."

He crouched by Aurora's side, his knees hitting the gravel harder than he'd intended. "Aurora?" He leaned close to her ear. "Aurora? Aurora! Wake up!"

Aurora didn't stir.

"Aurora, can you hear me?" He shook her shoulder.

Polk crouches beside Aurora as her body gushes dreams. It's like standing next to a broken oil well. Dreams tear the skin from his cheeks.

Polk fell back, staring at his throbbing fingers. *What am I going to do now?*

Find a way. Right now, I'm the only one who can. Do it!

He stumbled forward, then stopped when he brushed something that clinked on the gravel. He picked up the tarnished bronze knife Matron had given him, long ago. He ran his fingers over the ancient runes, and touched the blade, pulling his hand away as it pricked him.

The easy way.

He hefted the knife and looked at Aurora.

Not easy at all.

He dropped the knife.

The sky darkened. Polk looked up. There were no clouds, but the bright blue dome was deepening to midnight. At the edge of hearing, he could make out a deep rumble on the horizon, getting closer.

He felt something dripping down his cheeks and he touched his face. His fingers came away wet with blood.

"Aurora?" He leaned close. "Aurora, what do I do? How can I be Prince Charming if I don't know what to do?"

Then the words echoed back at him. *Prince Charming?*

He leaned over Aurora again and flexed his fingers. He grabbed her by the shoulders.

Dreams blast his chest and face, blowing him back, but he holds on. He looks down at Aurora and can just see her face, framed by dark, as though they were at either end of the inside of a tornado.

He leans forward, but her dark eyes open. He freezes, trapped by her terrible, sleeping beauty.

And then Aurora smiles. The weight behind her eyes is of someone who has swum miles across the ocean to the shore and needs just one pull to be free of the waves.

"You came," says her voice in Polk's head.

Polk smiles. He leans forward, fighting the force of her dreams, and he plants his lips firmly on hers.

The sound of rushing dreams cut off like a door closed on wind. Aurora's arms went around him, and she held him close.

Above them, the spiralling dreams faded, disappeared. The sky brightened. Polk and Aurora held the kiss as they felt the power ebb around them. When Polk finally let go,

Aurora looked up at him dreamily, the black vanishing from the whites of her eyes. Polk smiled. "Hey, Aurora. Wakey, wakey."

Then he fell back and lay still.

Aurora's eyes snapped open.

Aurora sat up, fully awake, and the world reeled.

Warm and steady arms gripped her shoulders as she almost fell back onto the gravel. "Aurora?" Her mother's voice. "Are you all right?"

Aurora moaned and waved off the helping hands. She kept her eyes closed and kept her hand over her mouth to keep from being sick. When she was ready, she reached out. Her mother grabbed her and helped her to her feet.

"Are you sure you're all right?" Dawn asked.

Aurora leaned on her, blinked once, looked around, then closed her eyes again. "My head hurts," she mumbled. She grimaced at the pasty-dry taste in her mouth. "Where are we?"

"We're back in Saskatoon," said Dawn. "On top of the bowling alley near my store. Everything's...okay."

Something about the way she'd said okay made Aurora look up.

Across the street, the pavement was drenched with water. The firefighters and the bystanders milled about, stunned, the bent, burnt and smoking cars forgotten. The people who had been in those cars now sat on the curb of the street, hugging their knees.

"What—?" Aurora heard the sirens echoing across the

city. She turned. Columns of smoke rose into the sky. "I did this."

Dawn gripped her shoulder. "Don't think about it. It's over now."

"But I...I did all this!" Aurora swayed. Tears trickled down her cheeks. "I'm a monster!"

Dawn grabbed her by the arms and looked into her face. "Listen to me! You are *not* a monster. You came back. You stopped yourself. That's all that matters."

Aurora looked away. "But...if it hadn't been for Polk..." She looked up. "Where is Polk?" She pulled herself from her mother's grip and turned.

Polk lay on his back by the parapet, arms spread-eagled. Matron knelt over him, her cheeks wet. Blood made two short red lines from his ears into his hair and dripped in small puddles on the roof.

CHAPTER ELEVEN:
AURORA AWAKES

A T Saskatoon City Hospital, the desk nurse looked up, exasperated, as the paramedics wheeled Polk through the admittance area with Aurora and Matron running to keep up. "Not *another* heart attack!"

"Not this time," said the lead paramedic. "Possible head trauma. He'll need an emergency MRI."

They shoved Polk's stretcher down the corridor. Aurora started after them but was brought up short by a security guard.

"Admittance desk, please," he said curtly.

Aurora slunk back to where Matron was waiting.

The desk nurse typed on her computer. "Patient's name?" she asked dully.

"Polk—" Matron began. Then stopped. "Polk..." The desk nurse looked up.

"Charmant," Aurora cut in.

The desk nurse's fingers clattered on the keyboard. "Your relationship to the patient?"

"He's my son," said Matron firmly.

Aurora said nothing.

"And how did he get his head injury?" asked the desk nurse.

Matron hesitated. Aurora spoke up, glaring at Matron. "He fell."

"Fine," said the nurse. "He's being assessed." She passed over a clipboard. "Fill out this patient information and find a seat in the waiting area." She nodded behind them. "Please be patient—it's been a long day. Next, please!"

Aurora turned towards the waiting area. She stopped short.

The waiting area was full, but strangely silent. People sat wherever there was space, many with arms folded across their chests, some hugging their knees. All kept their gaze on the floor. In the children's play area in the corner, a young girl sat, clutching her rag doll to her chest.

In the opposite corner, the television showed pictures of buildings on fire.

"...Scientists have no explanation for the epidemic of night terrors that swept the world and killed thousands," said the news anchor. "In other news, Russian factions continue to battle through the streets of Moscow, striving to fill the power vacuum left in the wake of the death of—"

Aurora reached up and turned the television off. No one objected.

She looked at Matron. Matron didn't look back.

"What happened to him?" Aurora's voice was dangerously quiet.

Matron gave her a glance, then turned away. "He'll be well looked after."

Aurora grabbed her arm. "What happened to him?" she shouted. People around them started to look up.

The automatic doors parted, and Dawn darted through. She ran over to the two of them, breathing heavily. "I'm parked. What's the news?"

Matron's face was red. "Don't do this. Not here."

"Answer the question!" Aurora shook her by the shoulders.

Dawn grabbed each of them by an arm and marched them outside. When the automatic doors closed behind them, Aurora pulled away from her mother's grasp and rounded on Matron. "What. Happened. To. Him?"

Matron studied the space above Aurora's ear. "You could see everything when you were the Dream Queen. I'm sure you saw what happened."

"You threw him into space!" Aurora yelled. "He fell to his death! But…but he woke up. He—" She faltered. "He kissed me. And then he keeled over?! Why?"

"It's as they say, girl: if you die in your dreams, you die in real life…if you're human. Fortunately, like you, Polk isn't entirely human. He can survive doing what he did… for a time."

Aurora felt the blood drain from her face. "He's not going to die!"

Matron looked at the ground. "I don't know."

"How could you do that?!" Aurora shouted. "You loved him like he was your own son!"

Matron looked up, her eyes blazing. "It was that or the world, girl! I had no choice! And neither did you!"

Aurora clenched her fists. Matron straightened up and

clasped her hands behind her back. Tears brimming, Aurora turned and punched the brick wall. Dawn darted over and pulled Aurora into a hug, but Aurora pulled back roughly.

"Go away, both of you," she choked. "Just...go!"

Dawn opened her mouth to protest, but Matron took her arm and pulled her back to the emergency entrance.

Aurora staggered into the parking lot, bumping into parked cars. She fetched up against a lamppost. She brought her knuckles to her lips and tasted blood.

She flexed her fingers and winced at the pain. Fishing through her pockets, she found a crumpled and matted paper towel and pressed it against her knuckles. She took a deep breath, held it and let it go.

What have I done to Polk? What have I done to everybody?

She leaned against the lamppost and looked at the sky. "What am I going to do?"

"What do you want to do?" said a deep voice.

Aurora started. She looked around wildly until she saw him. At the far end of the parking lot, parked across several spaces, stood the Dream King's black rig. The Dream King stood in front of it, looking at her across a row of cars.

Aurora pushed away from the lamppost and slipped between the parked cars toward him. She stopped twenty feet away and looked at him across an empty expanse of pavement.

"Hey," she said.

The Dream King bowed his head briefly. "Hey."

Another moment passed.

"Tell me something," said Aurora.

"What?"

She cleared her throat. "Am I a god asleep, dreaming that she is human, or am I a human who dreamed she was a god?"

He chuckled softly and looked away. Then he looked back at her. "Yes."

"Huh. Very helpful." She took a step forward, but the Dream King held out his hand, palm outward. "Come no closer."

She halted. "Are we gods?"

The Dream King leaned back. "We are…" He searched for the right words. "Elementals. Lords of Dreaming. The Dreamworld has existed alongside the real world since time mattered. Not only humans dream; dogs dream, cats dream. So do older things. The dream realm needs forces—guardians perhaps—to balance and contain the wild energies. We are those forces." He shrugged. "Your mother said that a man named Jung called us archetypes. How humans see us shapes what we are but doesn't change the fact that we *are*. We're here, travelling, watching, guarding. Sometimes interfering."

"Like me." She looked up. "I hurt a lot of people."

The Dream King sighed. "You could say it was just a dream."

"But it wasn't."

He gave her a sad smile. "You could say that you weren't yourself."

"But I was."

"What do you want, Aurora? Absolution? I can't give it. I'm as responsible as you. The fact we couldn't control ourselves is no excuse—at least, not to us."

She looked up at him. "Why did you come here?"

"To say goodbye." He fished through his pockets, finally pulling out a translucent globe and cupping it in his palm. "And to give you this." He tossed it to her.

Aurora caught it, then almost dropped it. It was heavier than glass, but the surface gave a little beneath her fingers, like rubber. The colours within shifted between clouds of blue, black and indigo, and within the clouds, she saw specks of light.

She studied it a moment, then looked up at him.

"Our people show up on that as specks of light," said the Dream King. "I used it to search for you. I found a lot of other people instead, all of whom told me to stop searching. You can use it to find more of your kind."

"Thank you." Aurora put the globe in her pocket and stepped forward.

"Stay back!" the Dream King shouted.

A spark crackled across the space between them. Aurora jumped back, and the Dream King pressed himself against his cab. Aurora waited for the world to end. It didn't.

She realized someone was holding her up from behind. It was Matron. Aurora shook her off and sat down heavily on the pavement.

Matron looked across the parking lot at the Dream King. "We tried to tell you, brother."

The Dream King closed his eyes. He nodded. "I should have listened. I need your help, sister."

"What can I do?"

He looked at the ground. "I have spent the last sixteen

years hunting. I've neglected my duties. The others of the dream realm have scattered themselves across the world. I have to go to them, apologize, and bring them home, if they want to come. But they don't trust me."

"I can help with that," Matron said quietly.

Aurora stumbled to her feet. "Matron! What about Polk?"

Matron looked at her, her lips tight. "There's nothing we can do except wait by his bedside. I'm needed elsewhere. I'll be back as soon as I can." She reached out and clasped Aurora's hands. "Can you keep an eye on him—take care of him while I'm gone?"

Aurora squeezed Matron's hands. "Count on it."

Matron gave Aurora a smile. Then she crossed the asphalt to the Dream King and hugged him. He grunted, surprised, held her a moment then gently pushed her back. "We should go."

"Wait," Aurora took a step forward, then back. "You should say goodbye to Mom."

The Dream King shook his head. "She won't want to see me."

"You're wrong." Footsteps rattled behind her. Dawn dashed up beside Aurora and stopped, breathing heavily.

The Dream King drew himself up. "Dawn?"

Without a word, Dawn darted across the distance and flung her arms around the Dream King. Aurora bit her lip and looked away.

"I've missed you," said Dawn, her voice muffled by the Dream King's shoulder.

"I've missed you too," he said.

She kissed him. Then she pulled away and walked backward until she stood beside Aurora once more. She took Aurora's hand.

The Dream King opened his rig door for Matron, who climbed in. He stepped up after her then stopped, his foot on the step, and looked back. "Goodbye, Aurora."

"Goodbye...Dad."

He climbed into the driver's seat and slammed the door. The engine roared to life. With a blast of its horn, it pulled out of the parking lot and onto the road, gathering speed. Aurora watched the truck until it vanished behind the distant buildings.

Somewhere in the distance, she heard the caw of a giant crow.

She felt her mother squeeze her hand. She looked at her. She yanked her hand free.

Dawn, pale-faced, reached out to touch her daughter's cheek, but Aurora backed away. "Why didn't you go with him?"

Dawn's mouth dropped open. "Why would I go with him, when there's you? We should—"

"We should what? Go back to our old life?" She shook her head. "Mom, I'm sixteen. Do you have any idea what I missed? I spent the last three years waiting tables and being homeschooled. My friends have moved on. I'm not the person I was when I was twelve."

"I know that!" snapped Dawn. "But I can't leave you on your own—"

"Why not?" Aurora shouted "I'm not a kid anymore. I'm not even human, anymore. I can take care of myself."

"Aurora, don't be silly—"

"*You're* the one being silly! The whole time I was with you, you never dated anybody else. You just sat at home. You love this man, and you're walking away to pick up something you...dropped three-and-a-half years ago?"

"I don't..."

"Tell me you don't love him!" Aurora squared her shoulders. "Go on, look me in the eye and tell me!"

Dawn's eyes flashed defiantly. Aurora looked into her mother's blue gaze.

...Dawn sets the infant Aurora in her crib and leans over as the baby coos. She smiles as she brushes back the silky curls...

...Aurora topples off her tricycle and scrapes her knee. She rolls up, bawling, and Dawn rushes forward to clasp her close...

...Aurora leans over her homework, her tongue in her teeth, so studious. But she smiles as Dawn leans close and kisses the top of her head...

...Dawn beams proudly as Aurora twirls at her ballet recital...

...Aurora sits on her bed, staring at her feet sullenly. Dawn stands by the door, wishing she knew what to say...

...Skipping stones in Lake Winnipeg. "A new world record!"

Aurora rolls her eyes. "Hardly."

"Well, who's to know?" says Dawn. "It's not like they keep records on that sort of thing."

"Actually, they do."

A crow caws...

Aurora broke the connection and hugged her mother. She grunted as her mother clutched her close.

"I loved him," said her mother into Aurora's ear. "I *love* him. But I love you too. Please let me take you home, hon. Or whatever home we can put back together."

Aurora drew back and looked into her mother's tear-stained face. She nodded. "Okay."

The heart monitor provided a steady background beat. Aurora realized she was stroking Polk's hand in time with it. She stopped. After a moment she began stroking in time again.

"Mom took me to her place," she said. "It's a basement apartment in an old house by the university. There's space on the top floor, and she's talking to the landlord about lending it to me until I can find a job to pay the rent."

Polk said nothing.

"It'd be my own place," she continued. "I'd have my own key and my own entrance and everything. Mom would be nearby, but, with an apartment between us, she wouldn't be looking over my shoulder the whole time. I could go to bed whenever I wanted. Or...not, as it happens."

The heart monitor continued its lonely rhythmic beat.

"Mom even offered me a job at her store. I'd handle the cash and the inventory, and she'd pay me enough to cover rent and food. Apparently, the place does well enough that she can afford it. And she wants to go back to school and get re-certified as a psychologist. She's even suggested that when she gets her license back, I could take over the shop full time."

She sighed and shook her head. "I never thought I'd end up owning a shop. I still have a few more courses to go before I get my GED. Not sure if I want to own a shop instead of going to university but...maybe."

She looked around the hospital room, over the fleece bedding, the darkened television set, the vase of drooping flowers by the window. The quiet pressed in on her.

"I got a letter from Matron," she said. "No stamp; neat trick. She's put the word out, and my father's people are starting to come home. She says she could be back later this week."

"I didn't write back," she added. "No return address." She let out a soft laugh. "Besides, I wasn't sure I was ready to tell her about her car."

Aurora looked down at Polk, whose mouth was slightly open. His eyes were closed, She closed her own eyes.

"Mom's given me a life," she said. "It's not what I had back in Winnipeg, but it's a life I could live. It's more than I deserve, but that doesn't mean anything to me as long as you're stuck here."

She cleared her nose with a sniff.

"I know I'm not supposed to tell you bad things, but—" She choked off a sob. "The doctors say there's no sign of brain damage. They say it's good news, but the truth is, they don't know what's wrong. They don't know why you won't wake up. And why would they? How many half-human dream lords have they ever treated?"

She clenched her fist but stopped herself before she hit the wall. "You're going to sleep forever, aren't you, Polk? It's not fair. You saved me." She sniffed again. "You pulled me back. Mom says I'm not a monster, but how can I not be? I made the world scream. And I put the one person I lo—I put him to sleep."

She thumped the wall, fist closed.

"This isn't the way it's supposed to go! Prince Charming's not supposed to be in a hospital bed. You're not supposed to—" Her breath caught. She tried to say it again. Failed. She let out her breath slowly. "You should have just killed me when you had the chance."

Polk's heart monitor continued its steady beep.

She leaned back in her chair. "You'd think being half a dream lord would be good for something. I mean, what kind of a dream lord would I be if I couldn't wake you up somehow..."

Aurora stopped chattering. She sat a long moment, staring at her toes. Slowly, she looked up. *How had I seen those dream curtains?*

She stood up and stepped to Polk's side. She looked down at him, brushing back his hair. Then she closed her eyes and took a deep breath. Then another. Then another.

Thank you, Dr. Zane.

Come to me, she thought.

She opened her eyes, looked down on Polk, and gave him a crooked smile. "C'mon, Sleeping Average. Wakey, wakey!"

She leaned forward and touched her lips to his. She held the kiss. She felt a spark.

Polk stirred beneath her.

She leaned back, her breath quickening. "Polk?"

Polk opened his eyes and smiled at her.

END.

ACKNOWLEDGEMENTS:
THE BOOK THAT GOT AWAY

B ACK IN LATE 2007, AFTER I HAD PUBLISHED *The Unwritten Girl* and *Fathom Five* and was finishing *The Young City* for publication, and as I was finishing the first draft of my urban fantasy *The Night Girl*, I hit on a new story idea. One of the oldest documents about this story featured the following notes:

- A daughter (Aurora), encountering something strangely mystical, doesn't realize how serious things are until her father takes her on a drive, and they drive all night and through the morning.
- The daughter is left to work as a waitress in a small-town diner. She wakes up and realizes she is in some sort of witness protection program.
- Who is she? Who is her father? What are they running from?

As you can see from the story before you, some things changed, but over the next eighteen months, this proved a fun story to write. Grabbing some welcome time while my toddlers played at the local Early Years Centre, I revelled in the free-for-all that dreams offered. I did ignore the truth that, in a surreal fantasy, you have to work twice as hard to keep your readers engaged and believing in the world since you are taking the rules of the world and throwing them out the window.

It was a more innocent time for me, but I was still pleased with the result, with *The Dream King's Daughter* becoming my fifth finished novel. This novel sat in reserve while I worked to get *The Night Girl* published before both took a back seat to my YA science fiction novel *Icarus Down*, which Scholastic Canada purchased and published in 2016. For the next book, while *The Night Girl* was not Scholastic's cup of tea (it was rewritten to become the new adult urban fantasy that would see print in 2019 and again in 2025), Scholastic did accept *The Dream King's Daughter* and announced the deal in March 2018.

Sadly, it was not to be. Staff shakeups at Scholastic Canada, as well as fallout from the COVID-19 pandemic, resulted in the book's cancellation (thankfully, Scholastic let me keep the advance they'd sent me), so I had no choice but to set *The Dream King's Daughter* aside while I worked to publish *The Night Girl*, and then finish the manuscript that would become *The Sun Runners*.

That was how a fully-written 55,500-word novel ended up sitting on my hard drive. This happens more often than you'd think. The unpublished novels of more famous writers could fill the largest library in history.

So, if I have this novel just sitting there, why not try again to get it published? Why not find a different publisher willing to take *The Dream King's Daughter* on? Well, for one thing, I'm not sure if *The Dream King's Daughter* is my story anymore. I am a very different writer now than I was in 2007. Compare the stories of *The Unwritten Girl, Fathom Five,* and *The Young City* to *Icarus Down* and *The Sun Runners* to see how I've evolved. While *The Night Girl* began in 2003, it underwent a from-the-ground-up rewrite that expanded the novel considerably, changing the narrative, the characters and the plot before it was finally published in 2019. The word count for *The Night Girl* grew from 64,000 words to over 90,000.

The Dream King's Daughter has not had the same opportunity, but while it would be tempting to give it the same treatment as *The Night Girl,* I have other stories to write. This isn't to disparage *The Dream King's Daughter*, which has a youthful energy about it that I find infectious in every good way, but I feel that it also stands as a window into how I used to be as a writer, which might be a useful thing to show, while also promoting my later works.

There are many people to thank for bringing this story to life. I am blessed to find myself in a vibrant and supportive writing community, including my critique partners at KidCrit. Particularly, thanks to Marsha Skrypuch who is a mentor to so many in the community, and I'm always grateful for her hard work. Thanks to Susan Fish who gave her own critique of this novel, and finished off the proofreading at the very end. Thanks to Sandy and Diane at Scholastic for believing in this book, even though they couldn't keep it. Thanks also to the Ontario Arts Council who supported the writing of this story through their Works in Progress grant, which was the first big win of my career.

Of course, I'd like to thank my family, particularly my parents; my father, Eric, was a great cheerleader, and my mother, Pat, offered excellent editorial advice. Thanks also to my in-laws for their great support and my partner in crime, Erin, for her love and lovely critiques. Thanks to my children for their patience and for sleeping long enough for me to finish the first draft.

Finally, thanks to you, the reader, for opening these pages. If I didn't have you as an audience, I'd just be a man talking to himself. Thanks especially to those who reach out, who comment and review, which show me that these important connections have been made.

Pleasant dreams, all.

ABOUT THE AUTHOR

James Bow writes science fiction and fantasy for both kids and adults. He's been a fan of science fiction since his family introduced him to *Doctor Who* on TV Ontario in 1978, and his mother read him classic sci-fi and fantasy from such authors as Clifford Simak and J.R.R. Tolkien. James won the 2017 Prix Aurora Award for best YA Novel in Canada for *Icarus Down*.

By day, James works as a freelance writer and communications officer. He also loves trains and streetcars. He lives in Kitchener, Ontario, with his two kids, and his spouse/fellow writer/partner-in-crime, Erin Bow. You can find him online at bowjamesbow.ca.

Other books by James Bow:

The Unwritten Girl
Fathom Five
The Young City
Icarus Down
The Night Girl
The Sun Runners
Tales from the Silence (as editor)